VANISHING ACTS

PHILLIP M. MARGOLIN

AMI MARGOLIN ROME

HARPER

An Imprint of HarperCollinsPublishers

ACKNOWLEGMENTS

We could not have written *Vanishing Acts* without help. Ashley Berman told us everything we needed to know about soccer, and Brian Ostrom helped us understand DNA and blood typing. Any mistakes about these subjects are our fault. Laura Arnold and Rosemary Brosnan, our intrepid editors, improved our original draft immensely, and we appreciate their hard work. We also want to thank Jessica Regel and Jennifer Weltz and everyone else at the Jean V. Naggar Literary Agency. Finally, our deepest thanks to Andy Rome for putting up with Ami, no simple task.

Vanishing Acts

Copyright © 2011 by Phillip Margolin and Ami Margolin Rome

Library of Congress Cataloging-in-Publication Data

Margolin, Phillip.

Vanishing acts / Phillip M. Margolin and Ami Margolin Rome. – 1st ed.

p.   cm.

Summary: In Portland, Oregon, between soccer games and beginning seventh grade, twelve-year-old Madison Kincaid and new classmate Jake try to track down her missing best friend, while also helping her attorney father solve a missing-persons case.

ISBN 978-0-06-188558-7

[1. Missing persons–Fiction. 2. Junior high schools–Fiction. 3. Schools–Fiction. 4. Soccer–Fiction. 5. Fathers and daughters–Fiction. 6. Lawyers–Fiction. 7. Portland (Or.)–Fiction. 8. Mystery and detective stories.] I. Rome, Ami Margolin. II. Title.

PZ7.M335662Van 2011   2011019379

[Fic]–dc23   CIP

                                                                           AC

Typography by Ann Zeak

12 13 14 15 16   CG/BR   10 9 8 7 6 5 4 3 2 1

❖

First paperback edition, 2012

This book is dedicated to Doreen Stamm Margolin,
a fantastic wife and fabulous mother. We miss her.

CONTENTS

PROLOGUE

Madison Kincaid could smell victory—she could taste it, she could even see it on the scoreboard where Lewis and Clark Elementary School, the Multnomah County champion, was beating its archrival, Prescott-Mather Prep, Washington County's best.

In less than two minutes, Lewis and Clark would be state champs for the third year in a row, thanks to Madison and her best friend, Ann Beck, the terrors of the elementary school soccer field since first grade.

There were two minutes left in this game, and the Prescott-Mather players were racing toward the Lewis and Clark goal to make a last-ditch effort to tie the score. Only that was not going to happen. Lewis and Clark had a top goalie in the net and Madison Kincaid in front of it. Best of all, Prescott-Mather had given the ball to Betsy Flint. Madison had played against Betsy many times, and Betsy knew that she was no match for Madison. Reading the uncertainty on Betsy's face, Madison foresaw exactly what was going to happen. Betsy would panic when the two girls closed and she'd take a desperation shot on goal. Madison would step in front of the shot, control it, then boom a kick to the other side of the field. And that would be that.

The play went *almost* exactly the way Madison thought it would. Betsy's eyes began shifting from side to side as Madison closed on her. Then Betsy hesitated. Betsy looked to pass, but all of her teammates were covered. She stared at the right side of the goal and kicked the ball exactly where Madison had predicted.

Madison had foreseen everything except the wet spot.

It had rained all morning, but the field had dried out by game time . . . except for one patch that was in shadow. One second Madison was racing toward the ball, and the next her feet shot out from under her and she was flying through space, her arms and legs shooting in all directions. Worst of all, the toe of Madison's right shoe connected with the soccer ball with such force that it sped like a bullet train into the left side of the Lewis and Clark goal.

Hitting the ground with a thud, Madison felt the air rush out of her. Her eyes squeezed shut. She couldn't breathe and she couldn't see. But she could definitely hear the screams and shrieks of the Prescott-Mather team, which was now playing in a tie game, thanks to Madison Kincaid. Her heart sank.

"Great goal!"

Madison's eyes opened. Staring down at her was Ann Beck's smiling face, rimmed by her unruly mop of frizzy blond hair. Ann always found something to smile about in the worst of circumstances. She held out her hand and pulled Madison to her feet.

"After the game, I'll explain why you're supposed to kick the ball into the other guy's goal, not your own," Ann said as they trotted up the field to taunts of "Wrong Way Kincaid."

"That's sort of catchy," Ann added.

Madison groaned. "We were so close to victory. I can't believe I did something so stupid." She felt embarrassed from the tips of her toes to her beet-red face.

"You just slipped. It could have happened to anyone."

"I let everyone down."

"Stop feeling sorry for yourself," Ann said. She gave her best friend a muddy hug. "We're still going to win."

As soon as the Lewis and Clark players were together, Ann called them into a huddle.

"These preppies think they've got us on the run, but they don't know who they're dealing with. We beat Prescott-Mather last year and we're going to do it again. We have a little over one minute to win the state championship, and 'Wrong Way Kincaid' is going to show Prescott-Mather the *right* way to do it."

Madison's teammates pumped their fists and shouted "Wrong Way, Wrong Way," to the great surprise of Prescott-Mather. Then the clock was ticking and Madison suddenly found herself with the ball, headed toward the Prescott-Mather goal.

The goalie focused on Madison, certain that she would keep the ball for a final shot so she could redeem herself. Three Prescott-Mather players formed up in front of Madison to stop her attack. The clock continued to tick.

Madison hid her hand by her side and gave Ann a thumbs-up. Anyone on Prescott-Mather who saw the sign would think Madison was signaling that she felt okay to take the shot, but this signal had been developed by Ann and Madison when they were in third grade.

Out of the corner of her eye, Madison saw Ann drift to the other side of the goal. When Ann was in position, Madison set herself to score. The Prescott-Mather players charged. At the last moment, Madison swiveled and kicked the ball toward Ann's head. Ann snapped her head forward, powering the ball into the net just as time ran out.

Screaming with joy, Madison raced over to Ann. They hugged and jumped in place as their teammates mobbed them.

"I can't wait for seventh grade!" Madison shrieked.

"We are going to rule Pettygrove Junior High!" Ann shouted back.

At that moment, Madison felt invincible.

"I WANT TO REPORT A MURDER!"

"**I** want to report a murder!" Thelma Bauer told the two policemen as soon as she opened the door.

Officer Jerry Kwong unsnapped his holster so he could get to his gun quickly. He looked like he expected a machete-wielding maniac to leap out at him. Officer Barry Jensen sighed. He'd forgotten to warn his rookie colleague about Thelma. Normally an order to investigate a murder had the effect of a double shot of espresso, but when Thelma Bauer was the complaining witness he reacted as if he was responding to a report about a missing cat.

Thelma Bauer was a sixty-nine-year-old retired bookkeeper who watched too many crime shows on TV.

Unfortunately, they gave her a view of the world in which everyone was a suspect, and she was constantly reporting suspicious behavior. Over the years, Thelma had reported several "criminals" who turned out to be gardeners, salesmen, and delivery boys.

"Tell us what you saw, ma'am," Kwong said.

After calling 911, Thelma had combed her short gray hair, applied makeup, and put on her nicest dress. She always made it a point to dress up when she phoned 911 in case television reporters followed the police. Thelma smiled at the handsome young policeman. Then she remembered why he was there and cast a nervous look at the house next door.

"We'd better go inside, in case he comes back," she said.

"In case *who* comes back?" Kwong asked as he followed Thelma's gaze.

"Mark Shelby, the killer," Thelma whispered.

Kwong and Thelma went inside. Officer Jensen hitched up his gun belt and pulled pants fabric out of his butt before following them.

The drapes were closed, but an old-fashioned floor lamp illuminated a floral couch covered in plastic; shelves full of snow globes, ceramic cats, and other knickknacks; and a forty-six-inch plasma TV that looked out of place among the dowdy furnishings.

"What makes you think Mr. Shelby is a killer?" Jensen asked.

"Oh, there's no doubt about that," Thelma answered with a confident smile. "Would you two like some coffee cake and tea?"

Kwong was about to accept when Jensen laid a hand on his forearm. The first time he'd answered one of Thelma's 911 calls, he'd made the mistake of accepting and had almost choked on the worst cake he'd ever tasted.

"Thanks, but we'll have to turn you down," Jensen said. "If a murder's been committed, time is of the essence."

"I understand completely. If a homicide isn't solved in the first forty-eight hours, the chances of it ever being solved begin to disappear," Thelma said, repeating the words of a wise detective from her favorite mystery drama.

"Exactly, Miss Bauer. So, why do you think a murder has been committed?" Jensen asked. Kwong whipped out a notebook and pen so he could take down Thelma's statement.

"I saw the killer getting rid of the body."

"Really?" Jensen said, fighting hard to keep the skepticism out of his voice. "Do you remember reporting a mob hit last year?"

Thelma blushed. "That was very embarrassing, but I

was certain that Mr. Bellini had been murdered by gangsters. In an episode of *Crime Busters*, the villain's henchmen rolled up a corpse in a rug when they were disposing of a snitch they'd bumped off."

"In real life, Miss Bauer, a pipe burst in Mr. Bellini's living room and the 'hit men' turned out to be carpet cleaners."

"This was no carpet, I assure you. I saw Mark Shelby put his wife's body in the back of his station wagon and drive away at high speed. Why would he peel out if he wasn't trying to get away from the scene of a crime?"

"You saw the body?" Jensen pressed.

"Not clearly, but he was carrying something that was the same size as Mrs. Shelby and I'd heard her scream just moments before."

"Why don't you start at the beginning?" Kwong suggested. "When did you first suspect foul play?"

"When their screams woke me up. And it wasn't the first time. This neighborhood was very peaceful until they moved in. The Shelbys fight all the time. Sometimes it's late at night, sometimes it's at dinner time. Today, they picked five o'clock in the morning and they woke me out of a sound sleep.

"My bedroom window faces their kitchen and there's only a thin strip of lawn to separate us. It was a warm evening and I kept my window open. I couldn't see much, but I could certainly hear those two shouting at each other."

"What did they say?" Kwong asked.

"I'm not sure. The kitchen window was closed. But they were both very angry. I did hear Ruth Shelby scream and I think I heard glass shatter. I thought he must be killing her. Then I heard the Shelbys' front door slam. I went into this room as fast as I could."

Thelma walked to the wall closest to the Shelbys' house and pulled back the drapes. Jensen could see the Shelbys' front lawn. At the side of the house farthest from them was a driveway.

"Their station wagon was parked facing out from the garage. The gate in the back of the car was down. Mark Shelby had his back to me. Ruth is a small woman and Mark is very big. I believe he played football. I could see he had something in his arms, and he was bent forward, like you would be if you were carrying a body. Then he heaved the corpse into the trunk, slammed the gate shut, and drove away at a high rate of speed, as if he was making a getaway. That's when I called 911."

"Did you check to see if Mrs. Shelby was home before you called 911?"

"Of course. I was afraid to go over there in case *he* came back, but I called their house." Thelma paused dramatically. "Ruth didn't answer, but I'd heard her scream just minutes before. All I got was the answering machine."

"We'd better go over and see what's what," Jensen said. He was certain that Mrs. Shelby would answer the door and he and Kwong could investigate real crimes or, better yet, go for donuts and coffee.

The policemen left Thelma's house and crossed the lawn. Jensen looked back and saw Thelma watching them. He rang the Shelbys' doorbell and waited patiently. When no one responded, he rang the bell again and knocked loudly.

"Police," he shouted after waiting for a response. When there was still no answer, Jensen tried the knob and was surprised when the door opened. Jensen frowned. This was suspicious. Why would the Shelbys leave the front door open if they were out?

"Cover me," he whispered to Kwong as he edged into the house with his gun drawn. He paused in the front room and listened for any signs of life, but the house was dead silent. Jensen looked around. The living room was clean and filled with expensive modern furniture.

"Bauer said the argument was in the kitchen," Jensen whispered. Kwong nodded. They moved down the hall in a crouch. Jensen felt butterflies flitting inside his stomach. He was too old for gunfights, and it was too early in the day to stumble on a corpse. Jensen loved to eat, but he knew he wouldn't be able to handle a greasy barbecue sandwich slathered with spicy red sauce if they discovered a dead body.

Jensen put his back to the wall on one side of the kitchen door, paused with his gun pointing up, and ducked into the room. Kwong followed. They lowered their weapons and stared.

"Something definitely happened in here," Kwong said. Jensen didn't disagree. The pieces of a shattered coffee pot were strewn in and around a puddle of dark brown liquid that covered a good part of the floor. There was another liquid on the counter that had seeped under the corner of a loaf of bread. Only this liquid wasn't coffee. There were also traces of blood spattered on the floor, and a fine spray decorated the ivory-white refrigerator door.

"Look at that," Kwong said, drawing Jensen's attention to the blood on the blade of a large knife that lay on the kitchen counter.

"Let's check the house," Jensen said.

Most of the Shelbys' home was as neat as the living room, but the bedroom was a mess. The bed wasn't made, and the covers had been thrown back as if someone had gotten out of bed in a hurry. The closet doors were open, too, and several items of clothing lay on the closet floor as if they'd been knocked down when someone was dressing.

"What do you think happened?" Kwong asked.

"I don't know, but I think we'd better find out what type of car Mark Shelby drives and its license number and have the dispatcher broadcast an all-points bulletin. I don't like all that blood in the kitchen, and I definitely don't like the fact that so much of it was on that knife."

2

A MIDNIGHT CALL

Madison was sleeping soundly in a soft, warm place when someone started burrowing into her head with a dentist's drill. Aargh! She rolled onto her stomach and wrapped her pillow around her head and over her ears, but the terrible sound wouldn't stop.

Madison used every ounce of her strength to raise an eyelid. The bright red numbers on her digital clock read 12:16. Groaning, she let her eyelid drop back in place. Last night she had been so excited about starting her first day of seventh grade that she hadn't fallen asleep until late, which meant she'd only been asleep for . . . Madison was so tired she didn't have the energy to subtract.

Brrrng! Madison struggled to a sitting position. She

was pretty certain she knew why someone was calling the Kincaid house after midnight. As much as she wanted to stay under her soft blankets, her curiosity wouldn't let her rest until she'd confirmed her deduction. Dragging herself out of bed, she tiptoed past her father's room with his still un-slept-in bed.

Madison's mother had died when Madison was in first grade, and she'd been raised by her father, Hamilton Kincaid. He was a top criminal defense attorney and a total workaholic. Once he got a case it became his life. It wasn't unusual for Madison's dad to work on a case deep into the night, and it definitely wasn't unusual for a new client to call after midnight.

The second-floor landing was across from her father's first-floor study. Peering through the railing, Madison saw that the door to the study was open.

"I'll be at the jail in half an hour, Mr. Shelby," her father said.

She ducked back from the railing just as Hamilton walked out of his den. Without looking up, he said, "I know you're listening, Madison. I have to go to the jail. I'll see you at breakfast."

Most of her friends' parents would never leave a twelve-year-old alone in the middle of the night, but Hamilton was absentminded, and Madison had grown used to taking care of herself. Double-checking that her dad had locked the door behind him, Madison, though curious, went back up to bed.

Madison's alarm went off at 7:15. She sat up right away. She was bleary eyed from her restless night, but if she hit snooze she wouldn't have time to blow-dry. Looking put together on her first day at a new school was seriously important.

By the second or third day, the snooze button would probably be in heavy use again. But today she couldn't afford to go back to sleep.

Grabbing her cell phone from her bedside stand, she speed-dialed Ann. Madison and Ann had met on the first day of soccer practice when they were both five and had been best friends and teammates ever since.

Madison often thought it was cool that two such different girls could be best friends. Madison was orderly, strong willed, and liked a plan, while Ann was happy-go-lucky and ready for anything. Madison loved school, though she knew it sounded dorky. She was a straight-A student and often read books that weren't required reading. She wanted to be the world's greatest crime-solving attorney, so she was always on the lookout for information that could someday come in handy. Sherlock Holmes, for example, could identify 140 different types of tobacco ash and had such a great knowledge of different kinds of soil that he could tell where a person had been by examining the dirt on the sole of a suspect's shoe. Those were just a few of the things Madison would have to know if she wanted to defend the innocent against unjust accusations in court.

Ann was smart, but she didn't read outside of class and didn't care if she got As or Ds as long as she could play soccer. Madison thought of Ann as her "head in the clouds" best friend. Ann probably thought of Madison as her "nose in a book" best friend.

With the first day of school also being the day of tryouts for Pettygrove's championship soccer team, Madison had to make sure she and Ann wore matching socks, a tradition they'd kept since the first day they met.

Weirdly, Ann's phone went straight to voice mail, so Madison left a message and rolled out of bed. After her shower, with her thick brown hair still wet, she threw her pajamas back on and went downstairs. On the way to the kitchen, Madison passed her dad's room. The bed still hadn't been slept in. It must have been a long night at the jail.

As Madison poured herself a big bowl of cereal, she heard her father working in his study. She carried the bowl into his home office.

"Hey, Dad."

"Morning, honey," Hamilton said without looking

up from the stack of papers he was reading. Though he had changed his clothes since the night before, his socks were mismatched and his hair looked like a hurricane had roared through it.

"It's the first day of junior high, Dad."

"Oh, yeah."

Hamilton finally looked up at his twelve-year-old daughter. She was tall for her age and thin, with strong legs from years on the soccer field. Madison knew her dad still had trouble thinking of her as anything but the little girl with pigtails who would color and play with her toys amid his law books.

Because Hamilton was a single parent who was addicted to his work, Madison had basically grown up in his downtown law office. When she was in elementary school, Hamilton would pick her up from school and take her to the firm. As she grew older and started to understand what her father did for a living, Madison began asking him about his cases—and giving him her unsolicited advice on how to win them. Eventually she became a file clerk at his office to earn pocket money, and by now she was addicted to anything having to do with law, including old Perry Mason novels and any lawyer TV show. The other kids in her elementary school would say they wanted to be bakers, teachers, and firefighters when they grew up. Madison wanted to be a criminal defense attorney and try murder cases. Now that she was entering junior high, she was more determined than ever to follow in her father's footsteps.

"New case?" Madison asked, munching on her cereal and pointing at a stack of police reports.

"Uhm," Hamilton grunted.

"What's it about?"

"Murder. A man named Mark Shelby is charged with killing his wife, but there's no body."

"Shelby? Mrs. Shelby was my second-grade teacher at Lewis and Clark. Remember?"

Hamilton's face scrunched up. He shook his head apologetically. "I'm not sure I do."

Madison was annoyed that her dad couldn't remember her second-grade teacher. His brain was so full of legal facts that there wasn't room for much else.

"Mr. Shelby's wife *is* an elementary school teacher, but I don't think he told me where she taught."

Madison put her spoon down, shocked. "Oh man," she said, horrified. "Mrs. Shelby was really sweet. Is he guilty? Is Mrs. Shelby dead?"

"Well, she might not be dead, sweetie, so please don't worry yet. My client says he's not guilty. He has no idea why he was arrested. And, like I said, there's no body."

"If there's no body, how can they arrest him?"

"Circumstantial evidence. If you don't have direct

evidence of a crime, like an eyewitness, you can still use circumstances to prove the defendant's guilt. Mark's neighbors have called the police several times because of screaming arguments. Yesterday, Mark and his wife had another argument. A neighbor claims she saw Mark put his wife's body in the back of his station wagon and drive off at high speed. When the police arrived, the house was empty; there were traces of blood on the floor in the kitchen and a knife with blood on the blade on the kitchen counter. Ruth Shelby is still missing."

Maybe the police had made a big mistake and Mrs. Shelby was okay. For now, all Madison could do was hope.

"Hopefully soccer tryouts won't take too long so I can get to the office to help you," Madison said, sobered.

"Tryouts, for a star player like you?" Hamilton said. "When the coaches see 'Madison Kincaid' on the list, they'll put you on the varsity without a tryout."

"Thanks, Dad," Madison said, rolling her eyes. "First of all, junior high doesn't have 'varsity.' You either make the team or you play club. And Pettygrove Junior High has won or placed second in the Junior High City Championship for the past five years. I just hope I make the team."

"You'll do great. Go get dressed and I'll drive you to school."

Madison ran upstairs and studied her face in the bathroom mirror. Thankfully, her pale skin was zit free. Not wanting to look like she was overly excited about her first day of school, she decided against any lip gloss, but she did blow-dry her hair. Today she needed her hair to be perfect to impress her new teachers and the other students.

When she was finished in the bathroom, Madison took out the outfit she had decided weeks ago to wear on her first day at Pettygrove Junior High. She was slightly bummed that Ann had been in Europe all summer so that she wasn't around to consult about what to wear. She put on a simple black tank top and pulled on her newish J. Crew jeans, which she'd broken in. Even though she was tall enough for them, talking her father into buying her grown-up jeans hadn't been easy, but she'd finally worn him down.

Madison felt like she'd been waiting for junior high forever. There would be new teachers, tougher classes, and extracurricular activities like debate club—perfect for someone like her who wanted to get a head start on lawyer skills. There would, of course, be a whole new crowd of boys and girls from the other elementary schools that fed into The Grove, and all of the eighth-grade boys and girls who would rule the school. That made her nervous.

To tell the truth, Madison admitted to herself, as she

brushed her hair again, she was never completely comfortable when she wasn't in a classroom or on a soccer field. In elementary school, she had been a soccer star and the other students assumed she was self-assured, but a lot of her confident air was a front. She was uncomfortable in social situations and never really felt that she totally fit in. A mother could have told her the way she was supposed to act with boys, but she didn't have a mom to confide in. And Hamilton was clueless outside of a courtroom.

That's where Ann came in. With her easy, friendly smile, Ann was at home in any social situation. Where Madison worried about saying or doing something stupid, Ann was spontaneous, and the right words always came out of her mouth. Everyone liked Ann, and with Ann by her side Madison knew she'd be okay.

Grabbing her cell phone, Madison tried Ann again. Right to voice mail. Weird; maybe Ann was sleeping in. Madison threw red, green, yellow, white, and black socks into her soccer bag to be safe, along with her well-worn black cleats, sweaty old shin guards, a shirt, shorts, a water bottle, and a snack of crackers and orange slices. Last but not least, she shoved the latest Max Stone legal thriller into her backpack.

Before she was ready to go, she picked up the picture on her night stand. "First day of junior high, Mom," she said to the photograph of a tall brunette. "Any words of advice?" Even though she didn't remember her mother all that well, Madison still found herself missing her, and often talked to her picture. Taking a deep breath, Madison put the photo back on her nightstand. Then she picked up her backpack and ran to her dad's office. After some cajoling, Hamilton gathered up his papers and followed Madison to the garage, where they got into his black Prius.

The Kincaid house was high in the southwest hills of Portland, and the view on the way down to the city was spectacular on a clear day. The Willamette and Columbia rivers divided Portland into an east side and a west side, and cars streamed over the eight bridges that crossed the rivers. In the distance, Mount Hood towered over the foothills of the Cascade Range. The mountain's snow-covered peak made Hood look peaceful, but every mountain in the Cascades was a dormant volcano. Mount Saint Helens had actually exploded in 1980, blowing out the side of the mountain and covering the city with ash.

The Grove was at the edge of downtown, a quick ride down the hill. They didn't talk much on the ride. Hamilton was busy thinking about his new case and Madison was nervous about the day ahead. As they pulled up, Madison craned her neck to see if she recognized any of the kids streaming into the school. She looked hardest for Ann or Ann's father's Navigator but didn't see either. Kissing her dad on the cheek, she jumped out of the car.

"Good luck today! And kick their butts at soccer!"

"Thanks, Dad! See you at the office when I'm done."

Hamilton drove off, and suddenly Madison was in the middle of a moving mob of junior high school students. She froze, a knot forming in her stomach. Madison had taken a tour of The Grove on sixth-grader visitor's day, but she had never seen it filled with a thousand students. Compared to her elementary school, it was huge. By sixth grade, Madison was a big fish at Lewis and Clark Elementary School, but here she was a minnow. Would she survive in these waters . . . or be swallowed up?

3

THE BULLY

The Grove had been built in the 1960s and looked it. The wide, locker-lined halls had ugly, red-and-puke-brown-patterned linoleum-tiled floors. Located on the edge of downtown Portland, it had a reputation for being the richest, preppiest, best-for-preparing-you-for-the-rigors-of-high-school public junior high in the city. Many of Portland's rich kids went to Prescott-Mather, the closest thing Oregon had to an East Coast prep school, but The Grove had its fair share of wealthy students as well.

An eighth grader's backpack knocked Madison out of her trance, and she realized that she should keep moving. She didn't want to pull her schedule out in the middle of the hall and look like some baby who had no idea where she was going, so she found the nearest girls' room and snuck into a stall. Her first-period class was Pre-Algebra in MH 102. *Okay*, she thought, *where's the math hall?* Luckily all seventh graders got a map of the school with their schedules. Memorizing the location for MH 102, she left the bathroom, trying to look like a confident girl who knew exactly where she was headed.

As she walked to the classroom, Madison searched the halls for Ann. She saw tons of casual friends from elementary school and greeted all of them with a smile and a wave. There was a lot of "How was your summer?" and "Can you believe we're in junior high?" but no Ann in the halls—or in MH 102. This worried Madison because they were at the same level in math. Then she remembered that there were a few sections of first year pre-algebra and decided she was being silly. The Grove was big and the day had just started.

By the time lunch rolled around, Madison was really worried about Ann, so it was a great relief to see Lacey, one of their friends from sixth grade, when Madison walked into the cafeteria. Lacey shrieked and ran to hug Madison, her blond ponytail bobbing with each step.

"Maddy! Isn't junior high the best? So much better than elementary school. The guys here are amazing. Love your jeans!"

"Um, thanks," Madison stammered. "Yeah, the first day has been okay for me. . . . "

"Grab your lunch. Jessi and Becca are already outside."

Madison looked down at Lacey's tray, which contained a salad and a diet Coke, then eyed the pizza bar. She should probably get a salad like Lacey, but she was hungry, and soccer tryouts were in a few hours. Grabbing a personal-size pizza and a carton of orange juice, Madison followed Lacey and her small salad outside.

Students were seated in clusters on the lawn, and surprisingly Lacey and her friends didn't look like baby sixth graders who had snuck onto campus. Madison said "Hi" to Becca and Jessi. She had been away at soccer camp and hadn't seen them all summer. Anyway, they were more Ann's friends than hers. Now, without Ann, she felt out of place. They chatted a bit about their classes before Madison got to talk about what was bothering her.

"Have you seen Ann?" Becca asked Madison.

"No, I've been looking for her all day. Has anyone seen her?" Madison asked. The other girls shook their heads.

"Hasn't she been in Europe all summer?" Jessi asked.

"Yeah, she's been traveling with her dad. But the strange thing is, she hasn't emailed, texted, or called me, even though she must be back by now, and I've left messages on her cell and emailed but never got anything back."

"She hasn't called me, either, and her Facebook is way out of date," Becca said.

"Yeah," Lacey added. "Her latest picture is way old, like from May."

"She probably couldn't email from Europe," Jessi said. "Do they even have email over there?"

"Duh, Jessi, of course they have email in Europe. It's not Mars," Lacey said.

"I bet something happened in Europe," Madison said worriedly. "Maybe she was kidnapped."

All the girls laughed.

"She was probably having a great time with French or Italian boys and was too busy to email or text back home," said Becca, who had actually kissed a boy and was the expert on anything to do with the opposite sex.

"If she was meeting boys, she would have definitely emailed me," Madison said, a pit growing in her stomach. "Something horrible might have happened. Her dad is a scientist and he's really weird. Maybe she was kidnapped by criminals who want a formula he discovered, just like Max Stone's *Project Murder*, where the daughter of the rich industrialist was kidnapped so the spies could trade her for the plans for the super computer."

"Honestly, who is this Max Stone?" Jessi asked. "Can't you read normal books?" Madison blushed. She adored the Max Stone novels.

"You always think the worst has happened," Becca said. "It's 'cause you hang out with your dad too much."

"Remember in second grade," Lacey chimed in, "when Madison announced to the whole class that Jessi had been murdered, because she had found a bloody Kleenex in the girls' room and Jessi wasn't in class?"

"And I was at the nurse's office because I had a bloody nose," Jessi said.

"That's not fair," Madison said, embarrassed. "You *could* have been murdered. Okay, maybe I was wrong about that, but this is serious. Ann could be tied up in a basement in London!"

"Or she just might have decided to skip the first day of school to get over jet lag," Becca said.

"Are you Madison Kincaid?" someone said.

Madison looked up and saw three eighth-grade girls standing over her. The biggest girl was the one who had spoken. She was two inches taller than Madison and twenty muscular pounds heavier, and she was giving Madison a look of pure disdain.

"Yes," answered Madison, trying to sound confident even though she was nervous.

"I hear you're supposed to be a hotshot forward."

"That's the position I play."

"Not any more. I'm Marci Green and I *own* that position, so you better get used to riding the bench, *if* you even make the team."

Marci's friends sneered at Madison. Becca, Jessi, and Lacey were silent, not knowing how to respond. Then Marci turned her back and walked away with her gang in tow. Madison could hear them laughing as they disappeared from view.

A NIGHTMARE AT SOCCER TRYOUTS

By the time eighth-period science rolled around, Madison had started to get the hang of junior high. She'd figured out where her classes were, where the seventh graders hung out, and where the eighth graders ruled. But she still hadn't seen Ann, and she was convinced that something bad had happened to her.

When you grow up in a house where a call from prison in the middle of the night is not an odd occurrence, and murder weapons are discussed over cornflakes, you tend to think the worst. And Madison was thinking the worst when she slid into a random seat in her eighth-period science class. She was so preoccupied with imagining ghastly scenarios that she only half heard the teacher drone on about how great science class was going to be—something she ordinarily would have been excited about.

"Hey," a voice whispered, "you okay?"

She looked up. The boy sitting next to her was tall and gangly with clear green eyes, a smattering of freckles across his nose, and ginger-colored hair that spiked in places and was pressed flat in others.

"I guess," she whispered back, not wanting to attract attention.

"What word is always spelled incorrectly?" he said. Madison was thrown off. She began cycling through words in her head, puzzled.

"Um, I don't know," she said quietly.

"Incorrectly!" he whispered. Madison was stunned for a moment and then, against her will, let out a giggle and rolled her eyes.

The teacher stopped talking and stared at Madison.

"I hope I'm not interfering with your tête-à-tête, Miss . . . ?"

"Uh, Madison. Madison Kincaid," she answered, feeling her face turn tomato red.

"And your gentleman friend is?"

"Jake Stephenson, sir," the boy answered.

"Well, Miss Kincaid and Mr. Stephenson, do I have your permission to continue?"

"Sorry," Madison mumbled. Ann was temporarily

forgotten. This really wasn't the way she wanted to end her first day in junior high.

As soon as science was over, Madison got up to hurry to the girls' locker room to change for soccer tryouts. As she walked out of the science class, someone tapped her on the shoulder.

"This is for you," the red-headed boy said as he handed her a folded piece of paper. Madison quickly opened the sheet. It was a goofy cartoon of the science teacher yelling at them. Madison grinned and looked up, but the cute red-haired boy was gone.

That was really weird, Madison thought. And it was confusing. Why had . . . she couldn't remember his name because she'd been too embarrassed by the teacher when the boy had said it. Did he want to be friends? Madison had never had a good friend who was a boy. Oh well, this was no time to think about something like that—she had to concentrate on soccer.

As soon as Madison got into the locker room, she pulled on her shirt, shorts, shin guards, socks, and cleats. Walking out to the soccer field, she couldn't help but notice that Ann was not among the girls trying out for the team.

"So you weren't nervous about junior high, you were worried about soccer tryouts."

Madison turned and found the same boy standing next to her, dressed in soccer gear.

"Oh, hi . . ."

"Jake. Sorry I didn't get a chance to introduce myself formally."

Madison liked Jake's southern accent, and he certainly had better manners than the boys at Lewis and Clark Elementary.

She found herself blushing. "I'm Madison."

"Yeah, I know."

"Thanks for the drawing."

"No problem."

"And I wasn't worried about school or soccer tryouts."

"Not concerned about soccer tryouts, huh? You must be pretty good," Jake said, smiling.

"I'm not amazing," Madison answered, embarrassed and blushing for the third time that day. "But I can kick a ball. I just don't want to be stuck on the bench this year."

"You'll do fine."

"What I'm really worried about is Ann. She's my best friend and I haven't seen her all day. We've been teammates since we were five years old, and she would never miss soccer tryouts."

"I'm sure she'll show up," Jake said, looking concerned. Madison thought he was about to say more when he suddenly got distracted by something that was happening on

33

the field. "It looks like tryouts are starting. I've got to go. Good luck."

Madison joined a group gathered around the girls' coach. Coach Davis was tall and gaunt with shoulder-length ash blond hair and a pale complexion. She was wearing sweatpants and a tee shirt, and she bounced a soccer ball in the palm of her hand as she spoke.

"Hello, ladies. Welcome to tryouts for the best junior high soccer team in the city. I see a lot of familiar faces. Good to see you back, Marci," Coach said, smiling at the eighth grader who had taunted Madison at lunch. "You ready to help our team win the city tournament again? Hey there, Ashley, Jennifer—good to see members of our winning team back for more.

"I also see a lot of new faces. I hope you're good—because our team is excellent and we won't take just anybody. I want to see great soccer today. Let's start so I can see what you're made of."

Coach Davis had the girls run laps before starting their drills. Then she led them to one end of the soccer field and made them jog in place. Every few seconds she called "Left!" and the girls had to reach down to the grass with their left hand. Then she'd call "Right!" then "High knees!" Starting to work up a sweat, Madison looked around to see who was keeping up and who was lagging.

This was the first soccer tryout she'd ever done without Ann to trade glances with.

For the next drill, Coach Davis got the girls in a line, told one of the eighth graders to guard the goal, then walked to the eighteen-yard box. The girl at the front of the line had to dribble twenty-five yards and pass the ball to the coach. The coach would then redirect the ball to the left or right and the girl would have to shoot the ball "one-touch" at the goal. It was her turn. Madison took a breath and focused. Her pass went straight to the coach. Then she timed the coach's pass perfectly, striking the ball with the laces of her cleats. She watched it sail past the goalkeeper to the upper corner of the goal. Madison wanted to shoot her hands into the air and shout, "Goal," but she knew better than to show off when she was trying to make the team, so she jogged away with her heart beating rapidly. Her eyes were down, but she could sense Marci glaring at her.

After a quick water break, Coach Davis set up teams for a scrimmage on a small patch of field outlined by bright orange cones. Marci was part of the five-girl team to which Madison was assigned. The goals were marked by more cones about four feet apart. A ball sat in the center of the field. When the coach blew her whistle, Madison raced toward the ball. She was almost to it when someone slammed into her side and she went flying. When she

35

looked up, Marci was kicking the ball through the goal. Then Marci turned, looked straight at Madison, who was still sprawled on the ground, and smirked.

"Great hustle, Marci," Coach Davis shouted.

Madison got up and brushed herself off. She was angry but couldn't give Marci the satisfaction of showing it.

"Good goal," she shouted instead.

Coach Davis mixed up the teams and Madison found herself facing Marci. When the whistle blew, she gritted her teeth and got to the ball first. Marci charged at her. Madison faked left. Marci committed and Madison shifted to the right, running around Marci. She was getting set to take her shot on goal when one of Marci's friends threw an elbow, catching Madison in the eye. On the turf again, Madison looked over at the coach, but she was bent over her clipboard making notes. Choking back her fury, Madison decided that the best revenge would be making the team. She would show Marci and her friends that she could take everything they threw at her and *still* outplay them!

The rest of the scrimmage was a blur. Marci and her buddies harassed Madison whenever they got the chance, but Madison did not end up on the ground again. She scored twice before the whistle blew and it was time for a break.

After a few more drills, the coach signaled the end of

the tryouts and the exhausted girls jogged back into the center circle and dropped to the grass.

"Great job, ladies, great job!" Coach Davis said. "I saw a lot of skill out there today, and I know we're going to have another championship team. I'll post the list of those of you who made the team on my office door tomorrow morning at eight a.m. Not everyone will make the team. Don't be discouraged if you're not on the list. Keep playing. I can give you the names of a few great soccer clubs where you'll be able to practice your skills and hopefully make the team next year."

Madison got up and brushed the grass off her legs. Club soccer! No way. She started to walk away. Then she remembered Ann. She ran over to the coach.

"Excuse me, Coach Davis? Is this the only time that people can try out? Like, if a girl missed it? Do they have a chance of making the team?"

"This is the only tryout, honey. The club teams take players all year. But serious players should have shown up today."

This wasn't good, Madison thought as she walked to the locker room. Ann couldn't play club soccer! She and Madison had been on the same team forever. They *had* to be teammates!

THE SHELBY CASE

Walking to her father's law office after practice, Madison imagined terrible things happening to Marci. Maybe she would be kicked off the team or break her leg. Yeah, that would be best. She would break her leg and have to sit on the bench and watch Madison score the winning goal in the championship game. Then Madison shook the thought away, feeling guilty. No leg-breaking. But someday Madison would show everyone how she could play.

Portland is a small city. The tallest buildings are no more than thirty stories high, and there are very few of those; and the city blocks are short. Kincaid and Kirk, her father's law firm, was in the heart of downtown.

Madison covered the ten blocks from The Grove to her father's office quickly, not stopping to look at the shops along the way.

The law firm's waiting room was decorated with oil paintings of French country scenes. Two comfortable armchairs flanked a burgundy leather couch, and magazines were stacked on end tables between the chairs and the couch. Walking to the dark-wood receptionist's desk, Madison saw Peggy Welles finish a phone call. Peggy was seventy years old and gray haired and had been working as Hamilton Kincaid's receptionist since long before Madison was born. She was the closest thing Madison had to a grandmother. When Madison was younger, it wasn't unusual for Peggy to pick her up at school and take her to soccer practice or the law office, since Hamilton was frequently in court, at the jail, or knee deep in work at two-thirty in the afternoon.

"Is this Madison Kincaid, the junior high school student?" Peggy asked with a wide smile. "How was your first day?"

"Okay."

Peggy took a gander at Madison's black eye and bruises, but she didn't freak out because she knew they were run-of-the-mill injuries for athletes.

"I take it you had soccer tryouts after school."

Madison nodded.

"I'm going to go get you some ice."

Peggy returned two minutes later and handed Madison a Baggie of ice and a towel.

"Thanks."

"Think you made the team?"

"I hope so. I'll find out tomorrow."

"Are you worried?"

"Not about soccer. I've had bigger things on my mind. I'm worried something might have happened to Ann. She might even have been kidnapped."

"Oh, really?" Peggy said, fighting hard to keep from smiling. This was not the first time Madison had decided that one of her friends had met a horrible fate.

"I haven't heard from her since she left for Europe, I didn't see her in school today, and she wasn't at soccer tryouts. She hasn't missed tryouts, practice, or a game since we were five!"

"Have you tried calling her?" Peggy asked.

"I've left tons of messages on her cell. And her Facebook page is way out of date. Becca, Jessi, and Lacey haven't heard from her either. Something awful must have happened. I'm sure she got some strange European illness and is in a hospital in Lithuania or she was kidnapped by—"

"I'm sure she wasn't kidnapped," Peggy said reassuringly. "There's probably a simple explanation for why she missed school."

Peggy was echoing what Madison's friends were saying, but Madison's instincts were telling her something completely different.

"Is Dad in?" Madison asked, wanting to change the subject.

"He's in his office."

"See you later."

Madison walked down the hall. The door to Hamilton's office was open, and she rapped her knuckles on the jamb to get his attention. Hamilton's office was as disorganized as his clothes. Papers were stacked seemingly at random on his desk, more papers stuck out from between the covers of the law reports that filled his bookshelves, and case files were spread across parts of the floor. Madison was always amazed at how such a sloppy person could be so organized in court. More than once, her father had astonished her when he broke down a witness with a razor-sharp cross-examination or cited a case, chapter and verse, from memory when he was arguing a legal point to a judge.

Hamilton didn't look up from his work when Madison knocked. To Madison it seemed that most dads would be dying to hear about their only child's first day at school. Some days Madison felt like Hamilton didn't even know she existed. She knocked again, harder.

Hamilton looked up, confused. "Hey, honey," he said, after registering it was Madison knocking. He didn't seem to notice her black eye. Inwardly, Madison sighed.

"Hey, Dad. How's the new case going?"

"It's coming along."

"Did you find out if Mrs. Shelby was my second-grade teacher?"

Hamilton sighed and rubbed his eyes. "She probably is, honey. She taught at your old school."

Madison was silent, crestfallen. Poor Mrs. Shelby. "I've never known someone who was murdered before."

"We aren't sure if she was murdered," Hamilton reminded her.

"So they haven't found the body?"

"No."

"In Max Stone's *The Spy Vanishes*, the missing CIA agent was hit on the head and got amnesia. Maybe Mrs. Shelby is wandering around and doesn't know who she is."

"I guess that's possible."

"Has the crime lab tested the blood on the knife yet? Maybe it's not Mrs. Shelby's."

"Maybe, but the crime lab says that the blood on the knife is Ruth Shelby's blood type."

Madison frowned. Then she cheered up. "Don't a lot

of people have the same blood type? Aren't there, like, only five, and most people have the main one?"

"Actually, there are four blood types," Hamilton said. "O, A, B, and AB, and they can be positive or negative. Mrs. Shelby is a B negative, which is the second rarest kind, and so is the blood on the knife. A little less than two percent of the population has that blood type."

"Two percent? That doesn't sound like that many."

"Well, yes and no. There are around three hundred million people in the US, so two percent of three hundred million is six million people."

"Wow, so it could be almost anyone's blood on that knife."

Hamilton laughed. "I wish you were on all my juries."

"Maybe someone with her same blood type came in and kidnapped her!"

Hamilton rolled his eyes, but kindly. "In a few weeks, when we get the result of the DNA test, we'll know if the blood is definitely Mrs. Shelby's."

"DNA tests take that long?"

"Yeah."

"And they really work?"

"They do. Only one percent of our DNA is different, person to person."

"So my DNA is ninety-nine percent the same as the president's or a movie star's?"

"Yup, but one percent is different enough," Hamilton said. "The police take a sample of the blood found at a crime scene and a sample of the blood of the victim. If that one percent matches, they have proof that the blood is the victim's blood, in this case Mrs. Shelby's. They also can test if the blood is the suspect's in the same way. The test is pretty accurate. The risk of matching a person's DNA incorrectly is one in a hundred billion if the test is done properly."

"If the police don't have Mrs. Shelby's body, what will they use to match her DNA with the DNA found in the blood?" Madison knew she was peppering her father with questions, but she was fascinated and wanted answers.

"They searched the Shelbys' house, and the forensic experts would probably have found hair or some other fluid that can be used for a match. When you live somewhere, you leave your DNA all over—hairs from your head, eyelashes, snot on the Kleenex you always forget to throw out."

"Yuck! And I do not leave my tissues all over! On TV they always take strands of hair from a hairbrush. That sounds easiest."

"That's true, but I didn't see a hairbrush listed on the evidence sheet attached to the search warrant, so they must be using something else."

"Well, if we find Mrs. Shelby alive we won't need

DNA or hairbrushes. Has Mark Shelby said if he knows where his wife went?"

"Madison, you know better than to ask that. A lawyer can't reveal what a client tells him in confidence. But enough about the case," Hamilton said, ending the conversation. "I have work to do, and you must, too. Why don't you start your homework in your office?"

Madison was frustrated that her dad had shot her down, and even more frustrated that he forgot to ask about her first day at school and soccer tryouts and that she hadn't gotten a chance to tell him about Ann. The Shelby case was absorbing him completely. Madison wished she knew a way for Hamilton to be as interested in her as he was in his cases.

Walking down the hall and through the file room, Madison came to the small, closet-sized room that had *Madison Kincaid* written on a plaque on the door. She had done homework in this office since she was little, but today she didn't start on her assignments right away. With her best friend and her second-grade teacher both missing, how could she think about math homework? She sat down at her desk and pulled out two legal pads, writing *Ann* at the top of one and *Shelby* at the top of the other. Maybe if Madison helped her dad solve the Shelby case, he would pay a little attention to her. She would finish her homework. Then she would crack both cases.

Madison's office wasn't very far from the reception area. With the door open, she could hear people talking, though she couldn't always make out what they were saying. Madison started on an essay for English class. She'd been working on it for half an hour when she heard Peggy ask her father about his visit to the jail to talk to Mark Shelby. Madison knew it was wrong to eavesdrop, but she couldn't help herself. She got up and crept as quietly as she could into the file room, where the conversation between Peggy and her father would be easier to hear.

"How is Mr. Shelby holding up?" Peggy asked.

"He's never been in jail before, and he's scared. Murder is the only charge where you don't automatically get bail, but I've scheduled a bail hearing for Friday and I think I have a good chance of getting him out."

Friday was a scheduled teacher-training day, and there would be no school. Perfect, Madison thought.

"What does he say happened?" asked Peggy, who was covered by the attorney-client privilege because she was Hamilton's employee. Unfortunately for Madison, the attorney-client privilege did not cover twelve-year-old volunteer file clerks.

"Exactly what the police reports say he told the detectives. He claims he forgot about his wedding anniversary and planned a golf outing with his friends. His wife was furious when she saw him getting ready to leave, and they had an argument. He says he was angry when he left and his wife was very much alive."

"Do you believe him?" Peggy asked.

"Yes, but . . . "

"But what?" Peggy pressed.

"I think he's hiding something. I just don't know what it is. But there's something he's not telling me. I have my investigator looking into it. There's something about his story that just doesn't add up."

Madison heard Hamilton move toward the door. She scurried back into her office and pretended to be engrossed in her work in case he looked in on her. But she wasn't thinking about her essay. She was thinking about Mark Shelby, and she was wondering what he was hiding from her father.

"HE'S CUTE"

The next day Madison had her dad drop her at school extra early. Walking into the gym, she could already see a crowd of girls gathered around Coach Davis's door, as well as a crowd of boys around Coach Chin's door. Some of the girls were smiling, but others looked sad and a couple were even crying. Before Madison had a chance to read the list, Ashley, an eighth grader who had been on last year's team, walked by her and said, "Nice job!"

Madison's heart rate went way up as she studied the list of sixteen players: eleven starters and five alternates. Marci's name was first on the list, and all but three of the names were eighth graders. None of the eleven starters were from the seventh grade, but Madison was number twelve, first alternate. Madison couldn't help grinning. She was the top seventh-grade girl in the school and had the whole season to prove that she should really be a starter. Then Madison sobered. This was the first time she had seen a roster with her name on it and without Ann's.

Before going to class, Madison took a quick look at the boys' roster. Jake was not among the boys looking at this list, but his name was third among the starters. Wow, thought Madison, the third best player in the school was a seventh grader. She was impressed.

Madison was still excited about making the soccer team when lunch rolled around. She saw Becca, Jessi, and Lacey in the same seats on the lawn as the day before, but she didn't join them. They'd always been more Ann's friends than hers, and Madison usually found herself feeling shy and being quiet as the other girls chatted away about boys and clothes. She would want to join in, but she had no idea what to say. Where was Ann? Madison needed her to pave the way with her bubbly attitude, as she'd done since they were five. Just one more reason Madison was missing Ann so desperately.

Taking a seat alone at the far edge of the lawn, Madison pulled out the latest Max Stone novel and read as she ate her lunch. As she was finishing, Jake walked over.

Sitting down, he pulled out the sketch pad he always carried with him. He tore off a piece of paper and handed it to Madison. It was a picture of Madison holding a soccer ball and watching the rest of her team play.

"Congrats on making the team!" he said with a smile as she looked at the picture. "First on the sub list is great."

Madison blushed, embarrassed by the compliment. "Thanks! I saw you were third on the boys' list. I'm sure a drawing of you would show you playing!"

"Yeah, well, I moved from Atlanta and I played on some pretty good teams back in Georgia. You must be less nervous today now that tryouts are over."

"I'm still worried about my friend Ann."

Becca, Lacey, and Jessi had been watching Madison talk to this new guy and had walked over. Madison wasn't always comfortable around boys, but there was something about Jake that made her resent the intrusion.

Hearing Madison mention Ann, Becca took the opportunity to jump into the conversation.

"Ann hasn't been kidnapped, Maddy."

Becca turned to Jake and smiled. Madison found herself feeling worried.

"Maddy always thinks the worst has happened. Say, Maddy, why don't you introduce us to your friend?"

"Sorry," Madison mumbled, annoyed but not knowing what to do. "This is Jake. Jake, this is Becca, and my other friends are Lacey and Jessi."

The girls smiled and waved.

"And I'm certain Ann is in danger," Madison went on.

"What Maddy is trying to say," Lacey interjected, "is that Ann hasn't shown up since school started. But we're sure she's okay. She's been in Europe all summer, and she's probably taking a few extra days before she comes back to the States."

Madison turned to Jake. "We met at soccer when we were five and made a pact to stay together through high school and win a state championship. There's no way she would miss tryouts."

"Missing tryouts *is* a very big deal," Jake said, giving Madison a sympathetic look. Madison felt her insides glow.

"And Maddy has a very active imagination," Becca said.

"That's because her father is a criminal lawyer who defends murderers and bank robbers, so she always thinks the worst," Lacey added.

"Your dad is a criminal defense attorney?" Jake asked, looking interested. "That's awesome." Madison looked up, a bit relieved.

Just then the bell rang.

"Oops. Got to go," Jake said apologetically. "I'll see you in science class. Nice to meet you guys." He ran off.

"You didn't tell us you had a boyfriend," Becca said.

Heat rose in Madison's cheeks. "He isn't my boyfriend. We just sit next to each other in science."

"He's cute," Jessi said as they gathered up their backpacks and headed inside.

Walking into science class, Madison was secretly happy to see that Jake had saved her a seat.

"Hi," she said as she sat down.

"Hey," Jake responded, looking serious for once. "I've been thinking. I want to help you find your friend. I've been playing soccer since I was six, and there is no way I would miss a tryout. Something bad must have happened to her."

Madison was surprised. No one else had believed her.

"That's what I'm worried about," Madison said as the science teacher started to talk.

"Let's meet after soccer practice to figure out a plan," Jake whispered, so the teacher wouldn't hear them.

"Perfect," Madison mouthed with a smile as she opened up her textbook. Jessi's right, she thought as she tried to pay attention to the teacher. He *is* cute.

PAYBACK

It had rained earlier that afternoon, and the field was muddy when Madison jogged out of the gym for the first day of soccer practice. Soccer was her outlet, her guilty pleasure amid all her academic hard work, and she was usually upbeat when a season started, but today her stomach was in a knot. She had never been bullied before and she felt anxious. She hoped that Marci and her gang would treat her differently now that they were teammates.

But over the course of practice it became clear that nothing had changed. Every time Marci or her friends had a chance, they would throw an elbow or try to trip her.

Her chance for payback came unexpectedly toward the end of practice. Coach Davis had broken up the squad for a scrimmage, and Marci and Madison were on opposite sides. Minutes before practice was set to end, Madison's teammate passed the ball to her. Marci grinned and charged. From the look on Marci's face, Madison could tell that she was aiming to end this encounter with Madison sprawled in the mud as she ran away with the ball she had captured.

Unfortunately for Marci, Madison had other plans. She saw her tormentor zeroing in on her and faked right, then changed direction at the last second. Marci tried to adjust to the fake, but she lost her balance on the slippery grass. Racing around Marci, Madison kicked the ball just beyond the outstretched fingertips of the goalie! The ball shot into a corner of the net, and Madison's teammates shrieked and pounded her on the back. Madison grinned. Then she looked over her shoulder and saw Marci struggling to her knees. Half of her face was covered with dirt, and her shorts were smeared with mud and grass. Madison was tempted to gloat, but she decided that scoring a goal while Marci was eating mud would send a message that Madison was not going to be bullied. If Marci wanted to keep her position on the team, the only way she could do it was by outplaying Madison.

☆　☆　☆

Walking out of the locker room, Madison saw Jake standing with a bunch of guys from the boys' team. Her black eye was pale yellow and purple by now, but she was sporting a fresh cut on her cheek courtesy of an intentionally thrown elbow, and there were more bruises on her arms and legs. Jake said good-bye to his friends and walked over.

"Are you on the soccer team or the boxing team?" Jake asked with his usual wide grin.

"I have a group of eighth graders determined to break my neck before we play our first game," she answered angrily.

"No way. If you broke your neck, then I'd have to find your missing friend by myself, and I don't even know what she looks like. So, have you called, emailed, and tried to get through on Facebook?"

Madison sighed. "Yeah, all of the above. Now I think it's time for me to try a low-tech approach."

"Huh?" Jake said.

"You know, actually going to her house," Madison said. "It's pretty close to school. Want to come? I mean, if you're not busy . . ."

"Sure," Jake said.

Ann lived in Northwest Portland, a section of the city on the northern edge of downtown. Hip boutiques and cool restaurants clustered on 23rd and 21st streets, and the surrounding area was populated with a densely packed blend of fancy old houses and apartment buildings. After an easy twenty-minute walk, Madison and Jake approached Ann's street. The houses were a mix of Victorians, Dutch Colonials, and other styles popular in the early part of the twentieth century, and all of them— except for one—had one thing in common: their lawns were mowed, their flower gardens were well tended, and none of them looked like they were in need of repair.

Ann's lawn looked like it hadn't seen a mower in ages, the paint on the siding of the house was peeling, and the place looked deserted.

"Does Ann's house always look like this?" Jake asked.

"No," Madison replied nervously, "it usually looks great. Ann's mom is always in the garden planting flowers and stuff, and her dad mows the lawn every weekend." She looked at the unkempt grass again. "Well, at least he used to."

"The house looks like it should be in a *Friday the Thirteenth* movie."

"Ann and her dad have been in Europe all summer. I guess her mom didn't keep the place up."

Jake studied the house. "It doesn't look like anyone's home."

Suddenly, out of the corner of her eye, Madison thought she saw a light in a second-floor window. But when she turned her head, it was gone.

"I thought I saw a light on upstairs," Madison said, "but I can't see anything now."

Jake followed her gaze. "In the daylight it's hard to tell."

They walked up to the front door and Madison rang the bell. After a few moments with no answer, she tried knocking. Then she called out, "It's Madison, Ann. Are you home?" There was still no answer. Shrugging her shoulders, Madison walked back to the front yard. The second-floor windows all looked dark, and Madison couldn't see the light she thought she'd seen before.

"I guess no one's home," Jake said.

"Yeah, it seems like it," Madison said miserably.

"Do you want to grab some pizza and figure out what to do next?"

"Sure. Let me call my dad and tell him I'll be late."

As Madison dialed her cell phone, she looked back at the house and thought she saw a window curtain move on the second floor. She was tempted to go back to the house and look around more, but Jake had already started walking away.

When they got to Amore Pizza, a popular hangout for Madison and her friends just a few blocks from Ann's house, Jake went to the counter while Madison found a booth. By the time Jake sat down with a small pepperoni pizza and two Cokes, Madison could feel her tightly wound nerves fraying.

"I think we need to go to the police," she said as she ripped a napkin into tiny pieces.

Madison remembered *The Spy Vanishes*. "What if Ann was hit on the head and is wandering around Europe with no memory?"

"Let's not panic. You said that Ann was in Europe all summer, right?"

"Yeah. Ann's dad is some sort of famous scientist. I think he was giving lectures over there."

"Maybe his lectures were so good that he stayed."

"Like they extended the trip or something?"

"Yeah."

Madison thought for a minute. "But Ann has to go to school. And why wouldn't she call me? Or email or something?"

She took a bite of her pizza. Jake's usually joking expression had been replaced with a thoughtful one. After a few quiet moments he looked up. "You said your father is a criminal lawyer."

Madison's mouth was full of cheese, so she nodded.

"Has he ever handled a kidnapping case? Maybe you should ask him about Ann."

"I dunno . . . Dad is so busy right now. He just got a

really hard new case." She took a sip of Coke.

"Oh yeah? What's it about?"

She quickly swallowed. "This woman called the police and said that she heard her neighbor being murdered. When the police went into the house, they found a knife and blood. And the most awful part is the missing woman is my second-grade teacher."

"Oh my God! I really liked Mrs. Haggard, my second-grade teacher," he said mid-bite.

"I really liked Mrs. Shelby too, and I can't stand thinking that something bad has happened to her. I'm so worried."

"Is there a chance she's alive?"

"No one knows for sure. They haven't found Mrs. Shelby's body, but they arrested her husband for murder anyway."

"Wow! That's like *CSI*," Jake said. "Have you ever seen a trial in person?"

"Oh, yeah," Madison replied casually. "I go all the time."

"Can anyone watch?"

"Sure!"

"I've never been in a courtroom. It would be pretty cool to go. . . ."

"There's a bail hearing for Mr. Shelby on Friday. That's a teacher-training day, so there's no school or soccer practice."

Jake was reaching for his third slice of pizza. Madison couldn't believe the words that came out of her mouth next.

"Do you want to come with me?" She ducked her head and filled her mouth with more pizza.

Jake flashed his wide gap-toothed smile. "That sounds great."

Madison was about to say, "It's a date," but she caught herself. Was asking Jake to watch a bail hearing the same thing as asking him out on a date? Dates were usually, like, going to movies or to the mall, so she wasn't sure. She decided that going to court would be educational, so it couldn't be a date.

"Is your mom a lawyer, too?" Jake asked.

It was the question she always dreaded. In a few seconds, her mood went from high to low.

Discussing her mom always made her sad. She guessed she'd never get used to not having one. One time many years ago, Madison and Peggy had had a serious talk about Madison's mother. Madison had been in a school play, and Hamilton couldn't come because he was in a big trial in California. Madison had been staying with Peggy, and Peggy had come to school in Hamilton's place. After the play, Madison saw all of her friends with a dad and a mom and she'd gotten teary-eyed. Until that day, Madison had accepted having a dad and no mom. She knew her mom was dead, but they had never really talked about it. On the ride home, she'd asked Peggy why other dads had wives and other kids had a mom and a dad.

"You had a mother, Madison. She was lovely, one of the sweetest women I've ever known."

"Why can't I remember her better?" Madison had asked.

"You were too young when she passed away."

"Some of the kids in my class have two moms," Madison said. She knew this because she had playmates whose fathers had remarried after divorce or death. "I'd like to have a mother, even if it wasn't my first mom."

Madison had seen tears form in Peggy's eyes before she turned her head back to the road.

"Your mother was so special that your dad hasn't found anyone to replace her," Peggy said.

"Does Dad work so hard because he misses Mom?" Madison asked.

Peggy looked surprised. "I think that's it," she said. "When your mother was alive, he didn't work nearly as hard. After she passed away, Hamilton buried himself in his work because he was very sad. I guess he never got out of the habit."

"Hey, you okay?" said Jake, waving a hand in front of her face.

Madison snapped out of her memories and looked

across the table at Jake. "My mom died when I was young," she said, hearing her voice go quiet.

Jake stopped smiling. He put his pizza down. "I'm sorry. I didn't mean . . ."

"It's okay. You didn't know. How about you?" Madison asked quickly, to change the subject. "What do your folks do?"

"They're doctors. They both work at OHSU," he said, referring to Oregon Health Sciences University, the hospital that had been built on a high hill overlooking Portland's city center. "That's why we moved from Atlanta. They got jobs here."

"What kind of doctors are they?"

"Mom's a cardiologist, a heart doctor, and dad is a neurosurgeon. He operates on brains."

"Do you want to be a doctor like your folks?" Madison asked.

"No. Their work is really interesting, but you have to be good at science if you want to be a doctor, and I am definitely not good at science. I really want to be a cartoonist or write graphic novels. But right now I just want to play soccer and make it through junior high in one piece."

Madison laughed. "I guess we don't have to make up our minds for a while," she said, but she'd known for a long time what she would be when she grew up.

8

THE MYSTERY WoMAN

The Multnomah County Courthouse was a blunt, eight-story building of gray concrete that took up an entire block in downtown Portland. On Friday morning the line to go through the metal detector stretched out of the courthouse and along the sidewalk in front of the building. In the line were intense-looking lawyers carrying attaché cases and making important calls on their cell phones, uniformed police officers who were scheduled to testify in cases, and nervous-looking men and women with greasy hair and dangling cigarettes. Madison tried to keep away from the nasty cigarette smoke as the line inched forward. She scanned the street, anxiously looking for Jake, who was late. Five minutes after they'd agreed to meet, a Volvo station wagon stopped in front of the courthouse and Jake hopped out. Madison waved and Jake ran over. He was dressed up for his first visit to court in a blue button-down shirt with thin white stripes and pressed khakis.

"Sorry I'm late," Jake said. "My mom made me change clothes when I told her where I was going. I feel like a dork in this outfit."

The exterior of the courthouse was brutish, but the lobby was an elegant mix of marble, dark wood, and polished brass. It would have looked nicer if it wasn't cluttered with metal detectors and guard stations. Madison had grown up in her father's law office, so she was used to mingling with suspicious-looking people. Madison watched Jake force himself to keep his eyes forward when two bearded bikers in black leather jackets and stained jeans crowded in behind him, then shift them toward the floor when he found himself looking at a skinny girl with glazed eyes and a nose ring and her muscle-bound, tattooed boyfriend.

After Madison and Jake made it past the airport-like security, they rode the elevator to the fifth floor, where Mark Shelby's bail hearing had just started. They tiptoed down the aisle and took seats on a hard wooden bench a few rows back from the low fence that separated the spectators from people having business before the court.

The Honorable Vikki Young presided in a grand, high-ceilinged courtroom with ornate molding, marble Corinthian columns, and a dais of polished wood. She was an intimidating, dour woman with jet black hair and piercing blue eyes who glared at the lawyers through glasses with Coke-bottle lenses. Madison really wanted to try cases . . . but she hoped Judge Young was retired by the time she graduated from law school.

"That's my dad," Madison whispered, nodding toward Hamilton, who was sitting at the heavy wooden counsel table at the side of the courtroom farthest from the empty jury box. Seated beside Hamilton was Mark Shelby. Madison studied him. He was a tanned, athletic man in his mid-thirties, thick necked and broad shouldered. He looked tall even sitting down. Madison only had to look at him for a few seconds to see that he was very nervous. Shelby was fidgeting in his seat, and his eyes darted around the front of the courtroom as if he expected to be attacked.

"Is that your dad's client?" Jake asked as they sat down. Madison nodded.

"I thought a murderer would look creepier," Jake said.

"Mr. Shelby is an *alleged* murderer," Madison corrected Jake. "Remember, accused people are innocent until found guilty."

"This guy looks too nice to have killed anyone."

"I know, most murderers look normal. If they all looked weird, it would be easy to catch them. But since they look normal, anyone could be a murderer—your dentist or librarian . . . anyone."

"Okay, okay, smarty," Jake whispered, smiling. "Where's the jury?"

"This is a bail hearing to decide if Mr. Shelby will have to stay in jail until the trial is over or if he can post bail and stay out. A judge decides whether to grant bail. You have juries at the full trial."

Before Madison could say anything else, a well-dressed African American in his early thirties stood up.

"The State calls Thelma Bauer," he said.

"Who is that?" Jake asked.

"He's Dennis Payne, an assistant district attorney. He works for the state, and his job is to convict people who are charged with a crime."

"Is he any good?"

"Dad thinks he's one of the best prosecutors in the District Attorney's office."

"Shh," someone behind them said. Madison turned to see an old lady shake her finger at them for talking.

"Sorry!" Madison whispered.

The courtroom door opened and the key witness in the case against Mark Shelby walked to the witness box. Thelma Bauer was dressed in her Sunday best and had applied too much makeup. She was just over five feet tall, but she stretched to her full height as she proudly took the oath to tell the truth, the whole truth, and nothing but the truth. Madison found herself thinking that Miss Bauer was relishing every second in the spotlight.

"Why don't you tell us what happened on the morning in question, Miss Bauer?" Dennis Payne asked.

Miss Bauer sat up straight. She looked very serious. "My neighbors fight all the time, but this time their screams woke me up at five o'clock in the morning. My bedroom is on the side of the house across from their kitchen, and there's only a thin strip of lawn to separate us. I had slept with my window open, which was unlucky for Mr. Shelby."

"Could you see what was happening?"

"No, I couldn't see much, but I could definitely hear those two shouting at each other."

"What were they saying?" the DA asked.

"I'm not sure. Their kitchen window was closed. I heard glass shatter, and I heard Ruth Shelby scream like she was being murdered."

Madison's dad leaped to his feet. "Objection, Your Honor."

"Objection sustained," Judge Young said. "Miss Bauer, it's my job to decide if there is a good reason to think

Mrs. Shelby was murdered. Just tell me what you saw and heard."

Miss Bauer reddened. She obviously didn't appreciate not being able to say anything she wanted. Madison smiled, proud of her dad.

"I *heard* their front door slam," she continued. "I can't see the front door from my bedroom, so I ran to the front of my house and looked out. I have a very clear view of their driveway."

"And what did you see?"

"Mr. Shelby's station wagon was parked facing out from the garage with the trunk open. That man had his back to me and he was carrying something in his arms. Something big." She paused for effect. "Something the size of a body. Then he put his poor wife in the trunk."

Leaning forward on her bench, Madison waited for another objection, but Hamilton's only reaction was a small smile.

"After that he slammed the trunk shut and sped away. That's when I called 911."

"Did you check to see if Mrs. Shelby was home before you called 911?"

"Of course. I was afraid to go over there in case *he* came back, but I called their house." Thelma paused dramatically. "I'd heard Ruth scream just minutes before, but she didn't answer. All I got was the answering machine."

Madison thought that Miss Bauer looked disappointed when Dennis Payne said that he had no further questions. When the prosecutor sat down, Hamilton Kincaid rose.

"Hello, Miss Bauer," Hamilton Kincaid said, flashing a friendly smile at the witness.

"Well, hello." Thelma answered with her own smile.

"We appreciate your taking time to come here and help the judge decide this matter."

"It's my civic duty to help the police."

"I'm sure they appreciate your help," Hamilton said. "In fact, you try to help the police a lot, don't you? How many times would you say you've called 911 to report a crime in the past year?"

"Oh, my, I can't remember the exact number."

Hamilton stood and held out a document for the judge's clerk. "Perhaps this exhibit will help you. It lists five calls to 911 in the past year. Does that sound right?"

"I guess so."

"You live in a nice part of town, don't you?"

"Yes."

"Most of the houses sell for three hundred thousand or more?"

"I suppose."

"Not exactly a crime-ridden slum, is it?"

"Oh, no, I have very nice neighbors. Or I did before

Mr. Shelby moved next door."

"We'll get to Mr. Shelby in a minute. But first, I'd like you to tell the judge how many of those 911 calls led to an arrest."

The witness looked uncertain and embarrassed for the first time. "I may have made a mistake or two, but Mr. Shelby was arrested."

"If we don't include Mr. Shelby, would it be correct to say that all of your crime reports turned out to be mistakes?"

"I, well, that may be true."

"Is it fair to say that you frequently *imagine* a crime is being committed when there is a perfectly innocent explanation for what has happened?"

"I . . . I guess so."

"Thank you for your honesty, Miss Bauer. Moving on, you testified that you saw Mr. Shelby carrying a body to his car?"

"Yes, he put it in his trunk."

"Did you see the body?"

"Well, yes. The car was blocking my view a little, but I could see he was carrying a body."

"Did you see a limb, an arm or a leg?"

"Well, no."

"A head or a foot?"

"No, but he definitely put poor Mrs. Shelby in the

trunk. May she rest in peace."

Hamilton nodded to the clerk and he rolled out a television set and positioned it so the judge, Miss Bauer, and the spectators could see the screen.

"I would like to show a brief video, Defense Exhibit Two."

"Objection," the DA said.

"We've been over this in chambers, Mr. Payne," Judge Young said. "I'm going to allow it."

Jake and Madison exchanged glances and leaned forward. Madison could feel the anticipation of the other people in the courtroom as well. Hamilton pressed Play on the remote and a picture of the front of a house appeared. A station wagon was parked in the driveway with the front of the car pointing to the street. Its rear gate was down, and there was a short space between the gate and the garage. Hamilton hit Pause.

"Do you recognize this scene, Miss Bauer?" Madison's father asked.

"It's Mark Shelby's house as seen from my front yard."

"And this is the view you had when you saw Mr. Shelby put his wife's body in the trunk of his car?"

"Yes."

Hamilton pushed Play and a man who was roughly the size of the defendant stepped out of the garage with his back to Miss Bauer's house. He was carrying something large, and he put it into the trunk of Shelby's car. Hamilton hit Pause again.

"Is this what you saw on the day Mr. Shelby murdered his wife, Miss Bauer?"

"Oh yes, that is exactly what I saw!"

Hamilton then pressed Play. The actor pulled the large object out of the car and showed a set of golf clubs to the camera.

"Wow!" whispered Jake into Madison's ear. "This is like a Max Stone novel!"

Madison's head snapped toward Jake. "You like Max Stone?"

"My dad loves those books. I've read a couple. They're pretty good."

Thelma Bauer's heavily rouged cheeks turned redder, and she gripped her skirt with her hands.

"That's . . . It was a body."

"You may have thought you saw Mr. Shelby put a body in his car, but might it not have been a set of golf clubs? A golf bag is about the size of a body, and you testified that you never saw any part of the body."

"I saw a body," the witness insisted stubbornly.

"I wonder when Miss Bauer had her eyes checked last," Madison whispered to Jake.

"Can you admit that you might have been mistaken?" Hamilton asked. "After all, it was early morning and you were awakened from your sleep."

Miss Bauer looked at the DA, but Mr. Payne was not allowed to coach his witness. He couldn't do anything but sit with a stone face.

"I guess it's possible," Miss Bauer conceded.

"No further questions, Your Honor."

"Anything more you'd like to ask, Mr. Payne?"

"I have nothing further of this witness," the DA said. "May she be excused?"

"Miss Bauer, you may step down," Judge Young said.

Thelma Bauer had looked confident and excited when she entered the witness box, but her head was down and her shoulders were hunched when she rushed out of the courtroom.

You got her, Dad! Madison thought. She loved watching her father take apart a witness, and she looked forward to the day her dad would get to watch her do the same. That would impress him way more than soccer.

"Your Honor," the district attorney said. "Before I call the next witness, I have an exhibit I'd like to offer. It's a stipulation between the parties that, if called, William Hubert, Jesse Marks, and Bruce Thomas would testify that Mr. Shelby spent the day of this incident and the two days following playing golf at a resort in southern Oregon. They would also testify that Mr. Shelby drove himself to the resort and the other members of the foursome did not see him until he arrived."

"What's a stipulation?" Jake whispered.

"Dad had these witnesses, and the DA was nice enough to agree that he and Dad would just tell the judge what they would say so they wouldn't have to take time away from work to testify," Madison explained. "They'll testify in person when there's a jury."

"It is also stipulated that it takes approximately four and a half to five hours to drive from Portland to the resort," the DA told the judge. "Attached to the stipulation is a map of Oregon showing the route Mr. Shelby took to get to the resort from his house."

"Do you agree to the stipulation, Mr. Kincaid?" The judge turned to look at Madison's father.

"Yes, Your Honor."

"Then call your next witness, Mr. Payne."

"The State calls Officer Barry Jensen, Your Honor," the DA said.

"Your dad sure made Miss Bauer look ridiculous," Jake said.

"Dad may have more trouble with this witness," Madison answered, her voice heavy with concern.

As Officer Jensen walked up to take the stand, the old lady with blue hair shushed them again.

"Who are all these people?" Jake asked, lowering his voice and looking around the packed room.

"Most of them are 'court watchers,' retired people who watch court cases for entertainment. See those three women over there?" Madison pointed discreetly behind her to a group of elderly women. "They show up every time Dad has a case. They're his fan club. And the younger people with notepads are reporters."

Madison was about to turn back toward the front of the courtroom when she noticed a slender woman with curly blond hair who was sitting in the farthest corner of the spectator benches. Her hair reminded Madison of Ann, but it was the fact that the woman wasn't taking notes like the reporters and was too young to be retired that kept Madison looking her way.

Officer Jensen began telling the judge what he had found when he arrived at the Shelbys' house in response to the 911 call. Madison returned her attention to the front of the courtroom.

"Once you found the crime scene . . . ?" the DA started to ask.

"Objection!" Hamilton said, rising to his feet. "The prosecution has yet to establish that a crime has been committed."

"Your Honor," the DA said, "there was blood all over the kitchen, including on the blade of a large knife, and Mrs. Shelby is missing."

"If a crime occurred every time blood was found on

a kitchen knife, the police would be at my house every time I tried to cut a bagel."

A few of the court watchers chuckled. Judge Young was not amused. She slammed down her gavel and glared at the spectators, but she upheld Hamilton's objection.

"What did you do after you found the knife and blood?" the DA continued.

"I put out an all-points bulletin for Mark Shelby's car. When he showed up a few days later, I arrested him."

"What did Mr. Shelby say when you told him his wife was missing?"

"He acted surprised," replied Officer Jensen.

"Did he have an explanation for why she might be missing?"

"No."

"Did he have an explanation for the way the kitchen looked?" the DA asked.

"Yes, he admitted that he'd had an argument with his wife because he had planned to play golf with his friends and he'd forgotten their anniversary. He said that Mrs. Shelby threw the coffee pot at him and he left in a huff. He said he put his golf clubs in the car, not a body. He also had no idea how Mrs. Shelby's blood got on the knife, the refrigerator door, or the floor of the kitchen."

"Now, Mr. Kincaid and I have stipulated that if they were here in court, the defendant's friends would testify that they played golf with him at a resort in southern Oregon and that it takes about four and a half to five hours to drive there from the defendant's house. Did I tell you about that stipulation a few days ago?" the DA asked.

"Yes."

"Attached to that stipulation is a map showing the route the defendant claims to have taken when he drove to the golf course. Have you seen it?"

"I have," Officer Jensen said.

"After I told you about the stipulation, did I ask you to do something?"

"Yes."

"What did I ask you to do?"

"You wanted me to drive from the defendant's house to the resort and see if there was any place along the way where someone could get rid of a body."

"Did you drive the route?"

"I did."

"Tell the judge the places along the way where the defendant could have gotten rid of his wife's corpse."

Officer Jensen looked at the DA uncertainly. "That's going to take a while, Mr. Payne. There were an awful lot of them."

"Instead of listing each one, why don't you summarize what you found?"

Officer Jensen turned to the judge. "I drove through

mountains with turnoffs for logging roads and camp-grounds. There were farmers' fields and the road goes along the coast, so you could toss a body off a cliff or hide it in a cave." Jensen shrugged. "If I wanted to ditch a corpse so no one would find it, there were plenty of places along the defendant's route I could have done it and still made my tee time."

"Your witness, Mr. Kincaid," the DA said.

Jake looked worried, but Madison knew her dad could handle anything.

"Thank you," Madison's father said, rising. "Officer Jensen, did Mr. Shelby appear to know why you were at his home?"

"No, sir. He acted surprised."

"How did he react when you told him his wife was missing?"

"He did seem shocked."

"Did you search Mr. Shelby's car?"

"Yes."

"What did you find in the trunk?"

"His golf clubs, a pair of golf shoes, other golf para-phernalia, and a suitcase."

"Was the trunk tested for blood?"

"None was found."

"Now, did Mr. Shelby tell you that Mrs. Shelby also had a car?"

"Yes, sir."

"Was it in the garage?"

"No, sir. A tan 2004 Camry registered to Mrs. Shelby is also missing."

"When you searched the house, did you find that anything else belonging to Mrs. Shelby was missing?"

"Mr. Shelby pointed out that some of Mrs. Shelby's clothes were missing from the closet in the master bedroom."

"So it is possible that Mrs. Shelby, after getting into an argument with her husband, just packed up and left?"

"Yes, sir, that's possible."

"No further questions."

"Any more questions, Mr. Payne?" the judge asked.

"Yes, Your Honor. Officer, did you do anything to try to find out if Mrs. Shelby went on a vacation?"

"We checked airlines, cruise ships, buses, etc. There's no record of Mrs. Shelby traveling. We also checked the local hospitals."

"This case has been all over the news," the DA went on. "To your knowledge, has Ruth Shelby called anyone to let them know she's okay?"

"No, sir."

"Did she show up at her job? Call for a substitute?"

"No."

"So, Mr. Shelby could have taken his wife's clothing

to make it look like she was on a trip in order to hide the fact that he'd murdered her?"

"Objection!" Hamilton said, springing to his feet.

"Sustained."

The DA smiled. His point had been made. "No further questions. The State rests."

All this talk about a missing woman made Madison start thinking about Ann again. Maybe she should just call the police so an officer like Officer Jensen could investigate.

After the morning recess, Hamilton presented his witnesses, who testified to Mr. Shelby's good character. Just before lunch, the judge decided to grant bail. Her decision rested on the inability of the prosecution to produce a body.

Madison knew that the police and her father's investigator were trying to find Mrs. Shelby or her corpse because the side that succeeded would win the case. Madison was torn between being worried about her former teacher and her dad's chances of winning the case.

"Your dad is tougher than any of the lawyers in Max Stone's books!" Jake said under his breath.

Madison was about to answer when she saw the woman who had been sitting in the back slip out of the courtroom. Madison thought that she looked worried.

Just then the judge adjourned court.

"Are you going to say hi to your dad?" Jake asked.

"He doesn't like me to bother him when he's with a client. Let's leave so we don't distract him. He'll probably be busy arranging to have bail posted as quickly as possible so Mr. Shelby can get out of jail. I'll tell him tonight that we were in court."

Jake wanted to eat lunch and Madison suggested the food court at the Pioneer Square Mall in the center of downtown Portland, a few blocks north of the courthouse. On the way over, Jake chatted excitedly about the bail hearing, but Madison only half listened. Something about the woman with the curly blond hair bothered her, but she couldn't put her finger on what it was.

Just before they sat down to eat, Madison figured it out. She was certain that the woman was not Mrs. Shelby, but she looked enough like her to be her sister.

THE GETAWAY

Beep.

Groggily, Madison looked at the clock.

Beep.

Eleven a.m. Wow, she'd slept late! She reached over and grabbed her cell phone.

Beep.

"Becca" appeared on the caller ID. Madison sat up, pushing her hair out of her face. She clicked the Talk button.

"Hello?"

"Hey, Madison, it's Becca! You sound sleepy. Are you still in bed?"

"No, I–I was about to get up anyway. What's up?"

"Well, Lacey, Jessi, and I are meeting in the mall food court at noon. I thought I'd find out if you wanted to come."

Madison thought quickly. She did have homework to do, and she wanted to think about the Shelby case. And look for Ann. But maybe it would be fun to go to the mall like all the other junior high girls did. Plus, it was really nice of Becca to invite her. Ann was always the one the other girls invited to go to the mall, and Ann usually passed the invite to Madison. It felt good to get the invite directly from Becca.

"Sure!" Madison answered, swinging her legs out of bed.

At seven that morning, the sound of the front door closing had woken Madison up. Even though it was Saturday, her dad was at the office.

"My dad's at work, so would I be able to get a ride with you?"

"We'll pick you up in forty minutes."

"Awesome. . . . Thanks, Becca! See you soon!"

Madison dialed her dad's office, but the call went straight to voice mail. She sighed.

"Hey, Dad," she said, "I'm going to the mall with Becca, Jessi, and Lacey today. I'll have my cell if you need me. I love you."

Snapping her cell shut, she went to the bathroom to shower.

The girls bought smoothies in the food court, then walked toward Nordstrom to look at shoes.

"So what's Jake doing this weekend?" Becca asked with a coy smile.

Madison blushed. "I have no idea," she said, stepping onto the up escalator.

"You should keep better track of your boyfriend." Becca giggled.

Madison's blush deepened. "He's not my boyfriend. He's just a friend."

"You hang out all the time; he always talks to you at lunch. He's either your boyfriend or he wants to be," Becca argued.

Madison wondered if Becca was right. Of all the girls Madison knew, Becca was the authority on boys. She had "gone out" with three boys since the fifth grade and even kissed Jason Tompkins after the sixth-grade graduation dance. Suddenly all thoughts of Jake and boys vanished.

Ann's mother was passing Madison on the down escalator.

At least Madison thought it was Ann's mom. It looked like the woman Madison had seen at every soccer practice and game since she was five, cheering on the sidelines—but something was different. Ann's mom usually wore professional suits or tailored clothes even on weekends, and had her hair up in a tight bun or French twist. This woman had Ann's mom's face but was dressed in a long, flowing gypsy skirt, and her long hair hung down in unbrushed waves.

"Mrs. Beck!" Madison yelled.

The woman turned, and her eyes locked with Madison's. For a second the woman looked startled. Then she flashed a forced smile and gave a tight wave.

Madison's escalator reached the top, and she ran around to the other side of the floor to catch the down escalator, ignoring the other girls' puzzled calls. She ran down the escalator, pushing past shoppers. When she reached the bottom, she scanned the floor for the woman. Radio Shack, Body Shop, Kay Jewelers . . . but she'd lost her.

When Madison got back to the top of the escalator, the girls were laughing.

Jessi was bent over, hysterical. "OMG, you ran off like a crazy lady!" she said.

"That was Ann's mom. I can't believe she ran away!" Madison said, embarrassed and confused.

"She didn't run away," Lacey said, giggling. "I saw her wave at you. She probably didn't know you were chasing her."

"No way. She had to have seen me run down the escalator. I bet she was trying to get away so she wouldn't have to answer questions about Ann."

"I'm sure she wasn't avoiding you," Becca said, rolling her eyes. "She may not have been Ann's mom anyway. I've never seen Ann's mom in an outfit like that."

"It looked like Mrs. Beck's hippie twin sister or something," Jessi said.

"That makes me even more nervous." Madison sighed. "Maybe she was in disguise so we wouldn't recognize her."

"I'm sure Ann's fine," Jessi said, annoyed by Madison's never-ending dramatics. "I'm sure everything is fine. Let's go look at shoes."

"Yeah, a little retail therapy will make you feel better," Becca added, giggling.

Madison gave a halfhearted smile, but she couldn't shake the worry. What could have happened to Ann?

10

MADISON FINDS A CLUE

When Madison walked out of the locker room after Monday's soccer practice, Jake was standing with a group of guys from the boys' team. He saw her and waved. Madison remembered what Becca had said about Jake being her boyfriend. Was he waiting for her outside the locker rooms or was it just a coincidence that they were there at the same time? Jake said something to his friends, then walked over to her.

"Hi," Madison said. For the first time she found herself nervous around Jake. Why had Becca ever said anything?

"What are you doing?" Jake asked.

"I'm going to my dad's office to do homework." She

felt impulsive. "Do you wanna come along? We can work on our science homework."

"Sure, I've never been to a law office before." Jake pulled out his cell phone. "Just let me call my mom and tell her I'll be late."

While Jake made the call, Madison thought about what she'd done. Had she asked Jake out on a date? No, they were just going to study, so this would be another educational experience, like going to court together to learn about bail hearings. Studying together would definitely *not* be a date, Madison decided.

"Hey, Peggy," Madison said as she and Jake walked into Kincaid and Kirk. "This is my friend Jake."

"Nice to meet you," Peggy responded, her blue eyes crinkling in a friendly manner.

"We're going to do our science homework in my office."

"You have an office?" Jake asked, impressed.

"Sort of. You'll see."

They walked through the file room, and Madison showed Jake where she did her work.

"It's like the Bat Cave," Jake said.

"It's not that great," Madison answered with a shrug. But she was secretly pleased that Jake was impressed.

"Hey, I just have a desk in my room at home!" he said.

He looked thoughtful. Then he held his hands in front of him as if he were framing a painting.

"Maybe I'll make you the star of my first graphic novel. You'll be a junior high soccer star by day and a crime-fighting superhero by night. This will be your secret lair."

Madison laughed and punched Jake's arm.

"Ouch." He faked pain. "You definitely have super strength." Then he said, "So what's the room with all the cabinets we just came though?"

"Oh, that's the file room. Lawyers use tons of files for their cases. Dad has files for evidence, police reports, testimony. The files in this room are for current or recently completed cases, but Dad also has files from old cases in storage."

"Is the file for the case where we saw the bail hearing out there?"

"Yeah."

Madison had planned on working on the case, but she'd been sidetracked by her investigation into Ann's disappearance. An idea came to her. She knew she wasn't supposed to look in her father's files because the information in them was confidential, but how could she help her dad solve the Shelby case if she didn't know all of the facts?

"Let's take a look at the evidence in the Shelby case

before we start on our science homework," she said.

"Okay."

Madison walked into the file room and Jake followed her. It didn't take her long to find the Shelby file, which was actually many files, filling up a whole drawer. Madison started pulling out files marked *Witnesses* and *Police Reports* while Jake watched.

"Oh, look at this," Madison whispered, showing Jake a page in the *Witnesses* file. "It's Thelma Bauer's address!"

"I bet she could give us information about the case that didn't come out at the hearing," Jake said.

Madison ran back into her little office, grabbed her *Shelby* legal pad and quickly wrote the address down before she returned the file to the cabinet.

"This will definitely help me solve this case," she said. "Let's split up these files and look for clues!"

Jake started on the police reports. "Hey, look at this," he said, pulling Madison away from a list of potential witnesses. "This police report says that a blood-covered onion was found in the trash, as well as ham, eggs, and a green bell pepper. Isn't that weird?"

"I'll write that down. It could be important," she said, proud of their detective skills.

Madison started looking through a file titled *Photographs*. The police had taken pictures of every little detail in the house. Flipping through shots of the kitchen, bedroom, and living room, she stopped suddenly when she came across a photograph of the fireplace mantel in the living room. She could see several items on the mantel, including a picture of two women in a silver frame. One of the women in the framed picture was definitely Mrs. Shelby, her second-grade teacher from Lewis and Clark Elementary.

Madison hadn't thought about second grade in a long time, but a flood of memories came back to her. The day her father forgot to pack her lunch and Mrs. Shelby comforted her and gave her some of her own lunch. The colors and decorations in Mrs. Shelby's room. I *really* hope nothing's happened to her, Madison thought.

She put her nose up to the picture. The other person resembled Mrs. Shelby and the woman who had been sitting in the last row during the bail hearing, but the photo was too small for Madison to be certain. Madison kept a magnifying glass in her drawer. It was one of the tools of the detective trade. She was about to get it when her father walked into the file room. He stopped in his tracks.

"Madison, who is this?" he said, pointing at Jake, "and what are you doing?"

"Um, Dad, this is my friend Jake," Madison answered, trying to keep her cool. "We were, um, we were just doing our homework. Jake's in my science class."

Jake forced a smile, since he was too scared to speak, and gave a little "hello" wave.

"Madison Elizabeth Kincaid, I am not stupid. The answers to your science homework are not in my files."

"Yes, well, Jake came with me to see the Shelby bail hearing. He had never been to a court case before and . . ."

"Yes?" Hamilton was getting impatient.

"So, uh, I was showing him how you have files in cases like the Shelby case, which he saw."

"You know you're not allowed to look in my files. You know lawyer's files are confidential. You know better than to read them."

Madison decided to come clean. "Dad, I thought I could help you solve the mystery of where Mrs. Shelby went."

When Hamilton spoke he sounded exasperated. "We've talked about this before. Murder cases are serious. They are not fun and games. Twelve-year-olds do not have the experience to solve a murder case. You need to stop snooping. Now put those files away and do your homework."

Hamilton shook his head and walked off.

"Wow. I thought we were done for." Jake let out his breath.

Madison looked away, too embarrassed to meet Jake's eyes. "I'm sorry about that," she mumbled. "But I was wrong. I know I'm not supposed to look through his files." She sighed. "I just wanted to help."

"Hey, don't feel bad. It was my fault. I should have known better than to ask about your dad's private files."

"No, you shouldn't. Your folks aren't lawyers, so you'd have no way to know they're confidential. I knew I shouldn't look, but . . ."

Madison's hands curled into fists and she gritted her teeth. "I just wish Dad would let me help him. He still treats me like I'm two years old. And I *can* help. I'm smart and I'm going to be a lawyer someday. I wish he'd trust me more."

"Parents are like that. They always think you're just this little kid, no matter what you do."

Suddenly, he brightened. "I bet he'd think about you differently if you solved the Shelby case."

"How am I going to do that when he won't let me see his files?" Madison asked, her frustration showing in her voice. Then she felt her face light up. "Hey, Jake, I have a thought."

"About the Shelby case?"

"No, about Ann. I bet that The Grove has files just like my dad's, but instead of being about cases they'd be on kids. Ann must have a file at school. Maybe if we can get into that file it will tell us why she isn't coming to school."

"That's a great idea," Jake agreed. "Now we have to figure out how to see the files without getting sent to detention or suspended."

Jake smiled. There was danger involved in hanging out with Madison Kincaid, but he'd definitely never had this much fun in school in Georgia.

THE FILE

The next day, Madison waited for Jake outside of science class. When he walked down the hall, she grabbed his arm and pulled him around the corner.

"What are you doing?" Jake asked, confused. "We're going to be late for class."

"I have an idea," Madison said, smiling. "The school has files on all students in the principal's office. Ann's file should be there."

"Yeah, so?"

"I have to skip class and you have to cover for me."

"What?"

"Okay, here's the deal," Madison said. "Jessi helps out in the principal's office this period, and the principal's office is where the school keeps our files."

"Why do you have to go this period?" Jake asked.

"It's the only time Jessi is there."

Just then the bell rang and Mr. Swanson stepped into the hall. Madison ducked out of sight but there was no escape for Jake, so he went into the classroom. Mr. Swanson called the roll and stopped when Madison didn't answer.

"Does anyone know what happened to Miss Kincaid?" he asked.

"Mr. Swanson?" Jake said, raising his hand. "I think she went to the nurse. She said she was sick and might throw up."

Several boys snickered, but Mr. Swanson ignored them. He did not want to clean vomit off his floor or smell it, so he made a note on the roll and completed his task.

Meanwhile, Madison was inside the principal's office trying to get Jessi's attention.

"What are you doing here?" Jessi asked as she came out to meet Madison. "Aren't you supposed to be in class?"

"Jessi, I need your help," Madison said, ignoring Jessi's question. "Do you have access to student files?"

"Um, sort of, I know where they are, but I never go into the cabinet. Why?"

"I need you to get Ann's file."

"No way! First of all I'll get in huge trouble. Second of all, why do you need it?"

"Ann's been gone for over a week. No calls, no emails. I went to her house and it looked abandoned. And you saw how her mom acted at the mall. Seriously, Jessi. Please help. I just want to look at her file to see if it has any clues to why she's not at The Grove."

Jessi stared down at the floor. Madison let her think. When she looked up, she didn't seem happy.

"Go back to class before we all get in trouble," Jessi said. "Then meet me back here after the period is over. If I have a chance to get the file, I will."

Madison slipped back into her seat in science class. Waiting for class to end was excruciatingly painful. Finally the bell rang and Madison and Jake ran upstairs to meet Jessi.

"Did you get it?" Madison asked, unable to contain herself.

Jessi handed Madison a photocopied sheet of paper.

"What's this?" Madison asked.

"That's it," Jessi said.

"This is everything in Ann's file?" Madison asked incredulously.

Jessi nodded.

Madison and Jake looked at the piece of paper. It

showed that Ann was registered to attend but hadn't shown up.

"I looked at my file, just for comparison," Jessi said. "I have tons of papers in mine. Schedules, doctor's notes for PE, stuff like that. But Ann just has that one sheet."

"Wow," said Jake. "This is stranger than we thought."

Madison had to rush to get ready for soccer, and after quickly throwing on her shirt, shorts, shinguards, socks, and cleats, she zipped out to the practice field. She was surprised to find both the boys' and girls' teams sitting together on the bleachers and the two coaches facing them.

"Hey," she said as she took a seat on Jake's left. "What's going on?"

"I have no idea," Jake replied. "I got out here a minute ago myself."

Jake turned to the kid sitting on his right, Kevin, a seventh grader who was on the boys' team and had gone to elementary school with Madison.

"Do you know what's up?"

Kevin shook his head no.

"Okay, everyone," Coach Davis said, bringing the meeting to order. "I don't think I have to remind you we are two of the best junior high soccer teams in the state, but traveling and playing other teams of our caliber costs money. The school board and principal prefer to spend money on new schoolbooks. This year they're buying new math books, even though math hasn't changed in the past thousand years and the old books would do just fine." Coach Davis gave a frustrated sigh. "So, the math teachers get their new books and our athletes have to sell candy bars."

Coach Davis pointed to a stack of boxes. "They're a dollar a bar. Sell as many as you can. Hit up your parents' friends, the people they work with, your neighbors, everyone you know. The more bars we sell the more teams we can play, and the better we'll be. Last year Marci sold one hundred bars. It's not surprising the best player is also the most dedicated to all aspects of the team."

Madison couldn't stop herself from rolling her eyes.

"Okay," Coach Chin, the boys' coach, said, "let's get out there and practice, and remember to pick up your boxes of bars on your way home tonight."

"I wish Ann were here," Madison told Jake as they walked to their practice fields. Somehow it seemed natural for Jake to walk by her side. "She'd be awesome at selling candy bars. She wouldn't let anyone say no. But between finding her, trying to solve the Shelby case for my dad, and homework, I feel like I don't have enough time to add door-to-door salesman to my résumé."

"Yeah, this sucks. But every team I've been on had to sell something. At least chocolate bars are better than wrapping paper."

Suddenly, Madison stopped walking and a smile spread across her face. "What?" Jake asked.

"I just had a great idea. We can sell candy bars *and* solve the Shelby case."

"Huh?"

"My father says that a good investigator or attorney should never rely on photographs of the crime scene or police reports and should always go to the scene of the crime."

"The scene of the crime doesn't seem so safe, especially in a murder investigation. Why would you go there?" Jake asked, looking nervous.

"So you can see what a place really looks like. My dad had a case where a person inside a house positively identified his client as the person who had burglarized her house. In the police report, the officer wrote that the witness was certain she'd seen his client standing in the door of the home. Dad went to the house at night. There was a bright light attached to the outside of the door that threw shadows across the face of anyone standing in the doorway where the witness said she'd seen his client. He brought the jury to the house and proved that it was impossible for the witness to have seen what she said she saw. Guess the verdict?"

"Not guilty?"

"Exactly."

"And you're telling me this because?" Jake asked, confused.

"We have Thelma Bauer's address," Madison said.

"You're not suggesting . . . ?"

A smile spread across Madison's face. "Do you want to go sell chocolate bars this weekend with me? There's a great neighborhood I've never been to, where a witness to a murder lives."

Jake was shaking his head incredulously, but he grinned. "I'll come, but I'm going to spend all night practicing karate."

MADISON VISITS A MURDER SUSPECT

Madison hopped out of bed Saturday morning buzzing with energy. Jake's mom was going to pick her up at ten and drive Madison and Jake to Mark Shelby's neighborhood, which was on the east side of the city, across the river from downtown. The Stephensons were new to Portland and wouldn't know one neighborhood from another, so Madison had told Jake to tell his mom that the Shelbys' neighborhood was a great place to hawk candy bars.

Madison found herself feeling nervous about meeting Mrs. Stephenson. She wasn't sure if Jake was her boyfriend or just a fellow detective, but she wanted to make a good impression in either case. Madison rushed through breakfast, took a shower, then spent a long time choosing an outfit. She thought about wearing all black—after all, she was on a spy mission—but quickly realized that she would look rather silly walking around in black in the middle of the day. She looked quickly through her closet. Hmm . . . fundraising for her school. She grabbed her new jeans and a Pettygrove Junior High Soccer T-shirt. No one would question her methods when she was wearing a shirt advertising the team for which she was fundraising.

When Madison was certain she looked just right, she glanced over at her mom's photo for approval, imagining her mom giving her the thumbs-up. Then she went downstairs to wait.

Hamilton had left for his office while she was eating, so she had the house to herself. It was only nine thirty. She had a half hour to figure out how to interrogate Thelma Bauer. She was lost in thought when a car horn startled her. Her candy bars were in the refrigerator. Grabbing them, she ran to the Stephensons' Volvo.

Jake's mother smiled at Madison and told her to hop in the backseat. She had a nice smile that went well with her bright blue eyes and reddish-blond hair. Jake, who was sitting up front, had stacked his candy boxes on the passenger side, so Madison put her boxes next to his and sat behind Jake's mom.

"Thanks for driving us, Mrs. Stephenson," Madison said.

"You're welcome. But I'm used to playing chauffeur. Jake's teams in Atlanta always had to have fund-raisers to pay for one thing or another."

Jake was quiet during the drive to Mark Shelby's neighborhood. Madison chalked his silence up to the fact that he was with one of his parents. Madison was usually quiet around her dad if she was with her friends. Who wanted parents knowing what you were up to?

Madison had looked at a map of the neighborhood on her computer. She told Mrs. Stephenson to drop them a few blocks from Thelma Bauer's house, and they agreed that Jake would call when they wanted to be picked up. As soon as Mrs. Stephenson was out of sight, Madison and Jake went to opposite sides of the block with plans to meet a few houses down at Miss Bauer's. They started knocking on doors. If Miss Bauer looked out of her window, she would see two neatly dressed junior high students selling candy.

By the time Madison and Jake approached Thelma Bauer's door, they had sold a whole box of chocolate between them, so their day looked like it would be successful even if they didn't solve the Shelby case.

"Let me question Miss Bauer," Madison said as they walked up the neatly laid out slate path that led to

Thelma Bauer's front door.

"That's fine by me," Jake agreed. "You've probably seen your dad do enough cross-examinations and read enough lawyer novels to know how to question a witness."

Trying to look confident, she rang Miss Bauer's doorbell. She cleared her throat when she heard footsteps approaching and fixed a smile on her face.

"Good morning," she said when the door opened. "My name is Madison and this is Jake. We're in the seventh grade at Pettygrove Junior High and we're selling chocolate bars to help our soccer teams. Would you like to buy some?"

Thelma Bauer perked up. "I love chocolate. How much are your bars?"

"Just a dollar, and it goes to a great cause," Madison said.

"I'll take three bars. Let me get my purse."

Thelma left for a minute and returned with a big red handbag. While Thelma went through her wallet, Madison faked confusion.

"This house looks familiar," she said, peering around. "Has it been on TV?"

Thelma brightened. "It certainly has." Then she lowered her voice. "There was a murder next door and I was interviewed about it by *two* TV stations."

"I thought so! This is very exciting. I've never met anyone who's been on television before."

Thelma looked embarrassed. "It was only for a minute."

"Were you nervous?"

"A little."

"Why did they want to interview you?"

"I'm the one who called the police!"

"You did!" Madison exclaimed. "Then you're a hero. What happened?"

"Come in and I'll tell you all about it! Would you like some iced tea and cake?"

"Thank you. That sounds lovely. We've been walking in the hot sun all morning and we're both hungry."

"Then sit down and I'll be right back."

"Great work," Jake whispered as soon as they heard dishes rattling around in the kitchen and the refrigerator door open and close. A few minutes later Miss Bauer reappeared, carrying a tray with two pieces of cake and two glasses of iced tea.

"Thanks for the snack," Madison said. "Can you tell us about the murder?"

"I certainly can."

Thelma could barely contain her excitement as she told the story Jake and Madison had heard in the courtroom. While she was talking, Madison took a bite of her cake. She stopped in mid-chew. She *was* hungry, but not hungry enough to eat this cake. It was awful. She washed down her bite with a swig of iced tea and put down her fork.

"Were you frightened?" Madison asked when Thelma finished. "I would have been scared to death."

"I was, just a little. But I knew I had to do my civic duty. No matter how frightened I was, I couldn't let Mark Shelby get away with murder."

"You're very brave," Madison said, egging her on.

Thelma blushed. "Anyone would have done what I did."

"Is that the window you looked out?" Madison asked, pointing at a window in the wall facing Mark Shelby's house.

"It is."

Madison looked around the room. "I don't see a phone. How did you call the police? Do you have a cell?" she asked.

"I don't like those things. No, I called from the kitchen."

"This is so exciting. I feel like I'm there on that morning. Could you show us where you made the call?"

Thelma led them out of the living room and into the kitchen, where an old-fashioned phone with a cord was attached to the wall. Madison went over to the phone and looked back toward the living room. A wall blocked her view of the window.

Madison glanced at her watch. "Oh, no. We have to go."

Thelma looked disappointed to be losing her audience. "But you haven't finished your cake."

"It was delicious, but if we don't go now we won't sell our quota of chocolate bars."

"Thank you so much," Jake chimed in. "It was an honor to meet a real hero."

"And thanks for buying the chocolate!" Madison said as they walked out.

As soon as they were on the sidewalk and Miss Bauer's door was shut, Jake spit cake into his hand.

"Thanks for getting us out of there without having to finish that awful cake," he said.

"Did you see what I saw?" Madison asked.

Jake frowned, puzzled, and shook his head.

"The phone," Madison said. "It's in the kitchen. Miss Bauer wouldn't be able to see the Shelbys' house when she was making the call to the police."

"You're right," Jake said. He pulled a small sketch pad out of his backpack and started to draw Miss Bauer's kitchen with the phone and the wall.

He grinned. "When I write my graphic novel starring

Madison Kincaid, superhero, this will be the first case you solve."

Madison looked down at Jake's drawing so he wouldn't see her blush. "This proves it. Miss Bauer couldn't see the house while she was on the phone. Anything could have happened while she was calling 911."

Turning toward Mark Shelby's house, she studied it for a minute, then started up the slate path to the front door.

"What are you doing?" Jake asked nervously. "Do you have a death wish?"

"There's something I need to see."

"Madison, he's out on bail, he could be home."

"I hope so."

"He might be a murderer!"

"There are two of us and it's broad daylight. I don't think he'll do anything and I really have to see this. Remember what my dad says about going to the scene of the crime? We would never have learned that you can't see Mr. Shelby's house from Thelma Bauer's kitchen if we hadn't gone into her house. Besides, he might buy some chocolate bars."

Before Jake could protest any more, Madison rang the doorbell. A few seconds later they saw movement behind the glass panels that flanked the door. Madison had a feeling that they were being studied through the peephole. She waited patiently, and a moment later Mark Shelby opened the door. He looked exhausted and pale.

"What do you want?" he asked impatiently.

"Hi, we're selling chocolate bars to support the Pettygrove Junior High soccer teams, and we wanted to know if you'd like to buy any. They're just a dollar a bar and it's for a good cause."

Shelby smiled a tired smile. "I could use something good like chocolate to cheer me up." He felt in his pocket. "Let me get my wallet."

As he turned to go, Madison piped up, "Could I use your bathroom?"

Jake looked shocked. How could Madison go into a suspected murderer's house?

"Sure," Shelby said, pointing. "It's down the hall."

Madison knew the layout of the house from the pictures she'd seen in her father's file. When Shelby was out of sight, she walked into the living room. The photograph she was looking for was still where she'd seen it in the crime-scene photo, on the fireplace mantel mixed in with family pictures. It was odd seeing a picture of one of her teachers in someone's house. Madison thought of her teachers as never leaving school, not having lives, houses, and husbands, or going missing and maybe being murdered. She fixed the picture in her mind before hurrying into the bathroom.

Madison waited an appropriate amount of time before flushing. When she got near the front door, she heard Jake say, "Thank you, Mr. Shelby."

Madison froze. Shelby hadn't introduced himself. If he realized they shouldn't know his name, they were cooked. She had to think of something fast.

"How did you know my name?" Shelby asked just as Madison walked into the entryway.

"Thanks for letting me use your bathroom," she said.

Shelby looked back and forth between Madison and Jake, and he didn't seem happy.

"He knew my name, but I never introduced myself. Are you two reporters for a school paper?" he asked angrily.

"Oh no, sir," Madison answered quickly. "The lady next door told us your name, Miss Bauer."

"What else did she tell you?"

"Nothing. Though she did look upset when we said we were going to come here. Don't you and Miss Bauer get along?" Madison asked innocently.

Shelby thrust out a hand holding four dollars to pay for the four chocolate bars Jake had given him.

"I think you two should go now," Shelby said sharply.

"Thanks for supporting our soccer teams," Madison said as she and Jake backed out the door as fast as they could.

"I cannot believe you pulled that off!" Jake spat out

once they made it down the street. "I thought we were goners for sure."

"I admit that was close, but it was worth it. I found a major clue!"

"Spill!"

"When we were in court at the bail hearing, there was a woman watching the trial who didn't seem to fit in. And she ran out as soon as bail was set. There's a picture of Mrs. Shelby and that woman in the house!"

"What do you think that means?"

"I don't know, but I bet she knows something. Why else would she be in court?"

"Now we just have to find out who she is."

SPYING

Madison was nervous all day Monday because The Grove was going to scrimmage Prescott-Mather on Tuesday. Knowing she wouldn't get much playing time as a reserve, she hoped she would at least have a chance to show the coach her stuff.

Prescott-Mather was a private school attended by rich kids. Since it was private, Prescott-Mather could recruit. Lewis and Clark Elementary School and Prescott-Mather had squared off in two of the last three elementary school championships, and Lewis and Clark had always played extra hard against any prep school because they resented the edge recruiting gave them. Beating Prescott-Mather for the state championship felt extra sweet. But Madison also knew many of the girls on Prescott-Mather's team because they were her teammates on the elite team she played on after the school season was over.

Adding to Madison's nervousness was the fact that it was her first big game without Ann. Jessi, Lacey, and Becca were starting to get as concerned as Madison by Ann's absence. Becca had told Madison that she'd called Ann several times and hadn't gotten through, and Lacey had checked Ann's Facebook page and found it still unchanged.

As soon as practice was over, Madison walked across town to the law office.

"Hi, Peggy, is Dad in?" Madison asked.

"He is, but he's with Mark Shelby."

Madison's heartbeat accelerated and she started to perspire. What if Mr. Shelby came out of her father's office while she was talking to Peggy? He would recognize her and tell her father that Madison had been in his house. Madison grabbed her duffel bag and sped toward her office.

"I'll work on my homework," she said over her shoulder. "Why don't you wait until Mr. Shelby is gone before you tell Dad I'm here?"

Madison knew not much got past Peggy, so she ran quickly down the hall. She didn't want Peggy to notice that the mention of Mark Shelby's name made her nervous.

Madison shut the door to her office so Mr. Shelby wouldn't see her. She tried to do her homework, but it was hard to concentrate knowing that her father and his murder-suspect client were just down the hall talking about the case.

There was a restroom next to her father's office. Once, years ago, when Madison was using it, she heard noises. When she looked up, she'd seen a heating vent over her head and realized that she was hearing people talking. She had never been able to make out the words that people in Hamilton's office were saying, but she thought that she might be able to hear them more distinctly if she climbed onto the toilet seat and pressed her ear to the vent.

Madison debated the pros and cons of listening in on her father's meeting with Mark Shelby. Her father had told her many times what a client told his lawyer was confidential. He would go ballistic if he caught her eavesdropping and would probably ground her for life. But she *was* helping her father, even if her help was unofficial. What if she heard something that she could use to solve the case?

Madison peeked out of her office to make sure that no one was in the hall. Then she scurried down to the bathroom and locked herself in. Opening the stall, she climbed on top of the toilet seat. Muffled voices floated toward her through the vent. When she pressed her ear to the metal covering, she could just make out what was being said. Her father was talking, and he sounded annoyed.

"We have a good chance of winning your case," Hamilton was saying, "but I've got to know all of the facts. If you're hiding something from me and the DA finds out before I do, he'll spring it on us during the trial and you could go to prison."

"I've told you everything," Mr. Shelby said.

"Let's go over what happened on the morning your wife disappeared one more time."

"It's like I told you. I got up and took a shower. When I was dressed I went downstairs. Ruth was in the kitchen. I told her I had a long drive and I appreciated her making breakfast for me. Ruth looked surprised, and she asked me what I meant. I told her I was spending the weekend with my buddies at a golf resort. She looked furious and asked me if I'd forgotten something. I didn't understand what she was talking about. She reminded me that this was our wedding anniversary weekend.

"I felt terrible and I apologized, but I said I couldn't let the guys down. Plus, we were staying at an expensive resort and I wouldn't be able to get my money back. That's when Ruth threw the coffee pot at me and started screaming. I didn't want to put up with her temper tantrum, so I left. She was alive when I drove away."

"What about the blood?"

"I have no idea how that got on the knife and the other stuff. There wasn't any blood when I left."

"And that's it, that's everything that happened?" Hamilton asked.

"Yeah, I swear," Mark Shelby said, but Madison didn't think that he sounded convincing. When her father spoke, she could tell he didn't think so, either.

"I hope so," Hamilton said. "I think that's enough for today."

Madison didn't wait to hear anything else. She jumped off the toilet and raced back to her office. She heard the door to her father's office open just before she closed her door. Then she fell onto her chair and took deep breaths. That was close, but it had been worth it. Madison was certain that Mr. Shelby had a secret, and she was determined to find out what it was.

Minutes later, Madison heard her father say good-bye to Shelby. She waited a minute before leaving her office. Peggy was alone.

"Did I just hear Dad?" Madison asked.

"He was showing his client out. I told him you were here. He said to tell you that he'd be another half hour. Then he'll take you home for dinner."

"Great."

Madison was about to return to her office when she remembered something.

"Peggy, what would you think of if I told you that I was in someone's kitchen and saw eggs, a green bell pepper, an onion, and ham on their counter?"

Peggy didn't expect the question, but it only took a moment for her to answer.

"That's easy. I'd think someone was making a Western omelet. Why?"

Of course, a Western omelet! Madison smiled. She was suddenly certain that she had just solved one of the mysteries in the Shelby case.

MADISON SEES A GHOST

Prescott-Mather was just over the line in Washington County and was not in The Grove's interschool league. The prep school had been the Washington County middle school champion three out of the past six years. Every year, The Grove boys' and girls' teams played a scrimmage against Prescott-Mather before the start of the season. Even though the game didn't count, the scrimmage was a big rivalry game because it gave the teams a chance to see how well they could do against top competition.

This year, the boys' game was at The Grove and the girls were traveling. Madison boarded the bus for the trip to Prescott-Mather and found a seat in the back of the bus with Gail, another seventh-grade alternate. Coach

Davis had made Marci team captain. Halfway to the prep school Marci stood in the aisle and gave a shrill whistle to get everyone's attention.

"Before we boarded the bus, Coach Davis told us to play hard today as if we were playing in a championship game. Well, I'm telling you to play harder than that. This game won't count in the won-lost column, but it counts here." Marci pounded her fist against her heart. "The players on Prescott-Mather think they're hot stuff because they're rich and go to a private school. Well, they're not hot stuff. That school recruits and gives out scholarships, and that's cheating as far as I'm concerned. Everyone who plays for The Grove lives near the school. We don't pick and choose. The Prescott-Mather snobs look down their nose at us because we go to public school. I say that makes us tougher. No one feeds us with a silver spoon. Today let's show those preppies where they can put their silver spoons." Marci's face turned red. "I hate the Prescott-Mather preppies. Let's crush them this afternoon."

Most of the girls cheered and whistled, but Madison was quiet. She'd never heard a coach or player on her elementary school or club teams say they hated anyone, let alone an entire school. As far as Madison was concerned, being angry hurt your performance. It was better to concentrate on doing your best. If you performed your fundamentals as well as you could, you'd play as well as you could, and it wouldn't matter if you liked or hated the other team.

Prescott-Mather had always been a big rival of her elementary school, but some of the girls on the two school teams played on elite club teams together and were friends. Madison couldn't imagine hating someone who was a teammate on a club team just because they played for a different school during the school soccer season.

The driver told Marci she would have to sit. She took her seat and everyone quieted down. Madison noticed that Coach Davis hadn't done anything to stop Marci or criticize her speech. She sighed. There was no question that Marci was the coach's favorite. Madison could see that taking her spot was going to be almost impossible.

The bus left the highway shortly after crossing the county line and headed into the countryside. Fifteen minutes later, it passed between two stone pillars with thick metal letters on them that told Madison that she had arrived at Prescott-Mather. A two-lane road passed between oak, maple, and Douglas fir trees for a short stretch before turning into the main campus, a collection of old stone classroom buildings and dorms for the students who boarded that would have looked at home at any Ivy League university.

The Grove's gym was part of the school building,

whereas the gym at Prescott-Mather was made of glass and polished steel and stood on its own plot of land. In the gym were a basketball court and an Olympic-size swimming pool. The soccer field was behind the gym and was surrounded by woods. The stands were filled with parents and students, even though the teams were only playing a scrimmage. Madison didn't look for her father in the crowd. She knew he wouldn't be there. Madison's father rarely made it to her games. She was sure if her mom was alive she would have made it to every single one of them.

The bus stopped and Coach Davis got off first. The Prescott-Mather coach was waiting for her, and the prep school players were lined up at her side. The coaches shook hands and chatted for a moment. They seemed like old friends. Then Coach Davis motioned for the team to get off the bus. The girls were already wearing their soccer gear. After they shook hands with their rivals, Coach Davis led them to the visitor's bench, where they huddled up and she gave them a short pep talk. Then she read off the starting lineup before sending the team out to warm up.

Madison was not starting, but she hoped that she'd get in the game at some point so the coach could see how well she played against a really good team. Thinking about playing against Prescott-Mather brought back memories of the last game she and Ann had played together. Madison blinked back an unexpected tear. For the first time in her soccer career she would be playing a game without Ann. Where was she? Was she safe? Madison would have given anything to know the answer to those questions.

With two minutes left, Pettygrove and Prescott-Mather were tied 1 to 1 and Madison was still on the bench because Coach Davis was only playing her starters. The coach looked more intense than Madison had ever seen her, and that was saying a lot. She stomped along the sidelines yelling at everyone, her face bright red. She was acting like this was the state finals. Madison had convinced herself that she would never get a chance to play when Carrie Metzger twisted her ankle and limped off in pain.

"Kincaid, get in there," the coach shouted. Jumping up, she raced onto the field. Her adrenaline was pumping. If she could just have the chance to get a shot on goal, the coach would see how valuable she could be to the team.

That chance came with a minute left. Marci had the ball and The Grove was moving upfield. Two defenders raced toward Marci, and she realized that she had to get rid of the ball. Marci looked to her left and saw that her closest teammate was being guarded. Then she turned to her right and saw Madison.

No one was between Madison and the goal because the defenders were concentrating on The Grove's stars. If Marci passed the ball, Madison would have a chance to score and win the game. Marci hesitated. Madison could read Marci's thoughts: The last thing Marci wanted to do was make Madison Kincaid look good, but beating Prescott-Mather was even more important. She faked one way and sent a beautiful pass toward Madison.

As Madison broke toward the ball, she calculated her next move. Only the goalie stood between her and victory. A short distance behind the goal was the forest. When Madison was inches from the ball, she saw movement in the trees.

Standing on the edge of the woods, staring at Madison, was a girl who looked exactly like Ann Beck.

Madison's mouth dropped open. She took her eyes off the ball and tripped over it. Her feet went flying and she hit the turf face-first. When she looked up, all she could see were feet racing by her. She pushed up to her hands and knees and saw players fighting for the ball, but all she could think of was the girl in the woods. Had she seen Ann or had her eyes played tricks on her?

Remembering the game, she leaped to her feet. Before she could get to the battling players, the whistle blew and the tie game was over.

"Thanks for nothing, you spaz," Marci shouted at her

angrily as she raced toward the bench. Madison hung her head. She had cost the team a chance to win. The other girls glared at her. Instead of being the hero, Madison was the goat.

When she got to the bench, Coach Davis gathered everyone around her and bawled them out for not playing hard enough to win. Standing on the edge of the huddle, eyes down, she expected to be the object of the coach's wrath, but Coach Davis ignored her, which was even worse than a tongue-lashing.

Prescott-Mather had set up a table with cold drinks and snacks. In a voice heavy with disgust, the coach told her team they could get refreshments even though they didn't deserve any kind of reward.

Madison headed toward the table, then veered off and streaked toward the woods. When she reached the spot where the girl had stood, she saw a path leading into the forest. She jogged along it. After a little while the path ended at one of the school's dorms. It was past five and she saw only a few students. None of them was Ann. She wanted to ask them if they knew Ann, but she had to get back to the team or the bus would leave without her. By the time she joined her teammates on the bus, Madison wasn't even sure if she'd seen Ann at all.

THE OUTCAST

All of the starters gave Madison the cold shoulder on the ride back to The Grove. To Madison's relief, Gail didn't protest when Madison sat with her again on the trip back to school. The other alternates were influenced by the starters and would not meet Madison's eye. When the bus stopped, Madison waited until everyone was gone before she got off. She was so embarrassed that she didn't want to be around the other players. As soon as her feet hit the ground, she headed for her father's law office.

Traffic was heavy because the people who worked downtown were driving home, but Madison was walking with her head down and she didn't notice. It was starting to get dark, and a chilly rain fell on her. She made no attempt to shield herself from the large, wet drops that soaked her hair and dripped down her face. The gloomy weather fit her mood perfectly. She couldn't believe she'd muffed her first chance to play for The Grove in such spectacular fashion. She wouldn't be surprised if the coach never played her again. Was it possible that her middle school soccer career had ended before it had a chance to begin?

As Madison reran the awful moments of her disgrace in her mind, she couldn't stop thinking about why she'd tripped over the ball. Was the person in the trees Ann Beck or had her imagination played tricks on her? Had she convinced herself that Ann was the girl in the woods because she missed Ann so much? She wanted that girl to be Ann because it would bring her a step closer to solving the mystery surrounding her friend's disappearance and make her humiliation on the soccer field a little more bearable. If the girl wasn't Ann, Madison had destroyed her soccer career for wishful thinking.

The waiting room at Kincaid and Kirk was empty when Madison walked in. It was late, and most of the employees and attorneys had left. Peggy looked up from her work when the door opened. She started to smile but stopped when she saw how dejected Madison looked.

"What's wrong?" she asked.

Dropping her duffel bag, Madison slumped on a chair across from Peggy's desk.

"I just made a complete fool of myself in our scrimmage at Prescott-Mather. The coach will probably keep me on the bench forever."

"I can't imagine anything that happened in a single game being that catastrophic, let alone in a scrimmage," Peggy said.

"You didn't see what I did," Madison replied gloomily.

"Why don't you tell me about it?"

Peggy listened carefully while Madison told her about tripping over the ball and falling flat on her face at the most crucial point in the game.

"You're not the only player on your team who didn't break that tie, Madison," Peggy said firmly when Madison was finished relating her tale of woe. "The other girls had the whole game to score a second goal."

"That's true, but I'm the only one who looked like a clown. On the ride back everyone treated me like I had a horrible disease."

"Don't make too much of one bad moment."

"You don't know Coach Davis. Beating Prescott-Mather is a big deal for her."

"Tell me about Ann," Peggy asked, obviously trying to get Madison's mind off her misery. "Are you sure she's the person you saw?"

"I don't know. I thought it was Ann, but she was far enough away so I couldn't make out her features for sure."

"And you lost her in the woods?"

"Yes. Whoever I saw must have been a student because the trail I followed ended at the school buildings."

"Can you think of a reason Ann would transfer to Prescott-Mather without telling you?"

"No, I can't think of any reason she'd switch schools. If she transferred, we couldn't play together. We vowed to be teammates forever and she'd know how disappointed I'd be." Madison felt her face scrunch up. "Besides, why wouldn't she *tell* me if she transferred? That's the kind of thing you would tell your best friend."

"Oh, honey."

Madison didn't want to cry in front of Peggy. Taking a deep breath, she straightened up.

"Why don't you put your mind to finding out if the girl you saw was really Ann?" Peggy suggested. "If she was and you find her, you'll get the answers to all your questions."

Madison perked up. "You're right. That's what I'll do."

An idea occurred to Madison and made her think about something else she wanted to discuss with Peggy. It was something embarrassing, but Peggy was the only woman she knew to whom she could open up about stuff that was personal.

"Peggy, there's something I want to ask you."

"Sure, anything," Peggy said.

Just thinking about what she was going to ask Peggy made Madison blush and look at the floor. It was times like these when Madison especially missed having a mother.

"How do you know if someone is your boyfriend instead of just a friend?"

"You're good at math, aren't you?" Peggy asked.

Madison nodded, a little confused by the question since it didn't appear to have anything to do with what she'd asked.

"In math, there are sure answers," Peggy said. "Four is always the answer to what is two plus two. Well, there's no formula when it comes to a boyfriend. It's something you feel. When you're around a boy or girl who is just your friend, you feel happy. When there's romance in the air, your heart soars and you feel giddy. And the two of you tend to act silly, but you don't care." Peggy smiled. "Is that any help?"

Madison's brow furrowed. She was definitely happy when Jake was around and she missed him when he wasn't, but she wasn't the type of person who acted silly or felt giddy. She was more the serious type. She decided that she was still uncertain about whether Jake was her boyfriend.

☆ ☆ ☆

Twenty minutes later, Hamilton knocked on Madison's office door. It was late, so they ate dinner at a small Thai restaurant near the office. During the walk to the restaurant, Madison thought about the game at Prescott-Mather and memories of her humiliating experience came flooding back. She was depressed by the time they sat down and ordered.

When the food came, Madison picked at it. Hamilton made small talk, but Madison responded with grunts. For once, her dad seemed to notice that something was amiss. Hamilton Kincaid was Oregon's best cross-examiner, and he finally pried her sad tale out of her.

When she finished, Hamilton started to laugh. Madison fumed, furious that her father wasn't taking her tragic situation seriously. At times like this Madison really missed having a mom. A mother would never laugh at something so awful.

"It's not funny, Dad!"

"Yes, it is. I can imagine how you looked flying through the air and landing on your nose. You just can't see the humor because you're too close to what happened. But let me tell you something. If I had a penny for every time I made a fool of myself when I was a young lawyer, I'd be a rich man. And I still make a fool of myself every once in a while. I just don't broadcast that fact.

"I can promise you that worse things than what happened to you today are going to happen. Screwing up is part of life. It's how you deal with the screwups that define you. You can either crawl in a hole and say, 'Woe is me,' or you can laugh at yourself, dust yourself off, learn from your mistakes, and forge on. This is a big deal for you now, but I'll bet most of the girls have already forgotten what you did because they're thinking about what they failed to do to win that game."

"You don't know some of the girls. They're really mean, and they'll never let me forget."

"Those girls are losers, Maddy. People who have to make fun of other people to feel good usually don't feel that good about themselves. You can put this behind you if you see the humor in what happened and learn from your mistake."

Hamilton's words didn't cheer up Madison at first, but the more she thought about what he'd said, the more sense it made. She remembered when she'd scored the goal against her own team in the championship game last summer. She almost never thought about that now, and what she'd done then was far worse than what had happened at Prescott-Mather. In fact, she took great satisfaction from the way she'd blocked out the wrong-way goal and sucked it up to help win the game. For the first time since the scrimmage, Madison smiled.

16

MADISON SURVIVES

Jake was waiting for Madison at the front door when she got to school the next morning.

"How are you doing?" he asked.

"So you heard?" she asked sheepishly.

"About your soccer debut? Yeah. A few of the girls were gabbing about it."

Jake handed her a drawing that showed Madison flying through the air with a goofy expression on her face. She couldn't help laughing.

"I must have looked pretty stupid, but I'm over it," she said. She wanted to appear confident to Jake even if it was only partly true. "And you'll understand why when I tell you why I tripped over that ball."

Madison told Jake about the girl she'd seen in the woods.

"Do you think she was really Ann?" Jake asked when Madison was through.

"I think it's possible. And I've thought of something I can do to find out if I'm right or wrong."

"What's that?"

"I'm going to take the bus out to Prescott-Mather and show a picture of Ann around. If she's a student, someone will recognize her."

Going to soccer practice was one of the hardest things Madison had ever done. When Marci spotted Madison in front of her locker, she sneered.

"I'm surprised you showed up today," she said.

Madison had expected Marci to harass her, and she'd decided how she would deal with her tormentor. Instead of looking embarrassed, Madison looked Marci in the eye and smiled.

"I sure made an ass out of myself, Marci. And I especially feel bad because your pass to me was so perfect. Thanks for showing enough confidence in me to make it. That meant a lot to me."

Marci hadn't been prepared to be praised by her rival, and she was speechless for a second.

"Well, pay more attention the next time" was the best

she could do. Then she turned away and led her buddies to the practice field.

Madison had anticipated a comment or two from Coach Davis, but the coach simply went over problems she saw with everyone's play and didn't single out Madison. Then it was practice as usual. By the time practice ended, Madison was starting to think that she might survive her horrible mistake after all.

FOUND!

The next day, Madison developed a really bad cold just before Hamilton left for work. Hamilton was too distracted to examine his daughter carefully, and as he walked out the door, he told her to drink plenty of tea with honey and stay in bed. She felt guilty about tricking her father, but she thought it was necessary if she was going to solve the mystery of her best friend's disappearance. Shortly after Hamilton left, Madison dressed and rushed to the stop where she could catch the bus to Prescott-Mather. Safely stowed in her backpack was a picture of Ann posing with Madison at a soccer game.

The bus stopped at the gate to the prep school forty-five minutes after she'd boarded it. Several of the riders were students at the school, and Madison mixed with them as they walked down the lane that led from the gate to the campus. Fishing Ann's picture out of her backpack, she showed it to some of the kids, but no one recognized Ann.

Students were streaming into class when Madison arrived at a quadrangle made up of a large, open grassy space surrounded by school buildings. She was approaching another girl when she saw a mop of frizzy blond hair out of the corner of her eye. Madison turned around and found herself staring at Ann Beck.

"Ann!"

Her friend stared for a second before sprinting away.

"Wait!" Madison shouted as she took off after Ann.

Ann had always been faster than Madison, and Ann also knew the layout of Prescott-Mather. She rushed around the side of a building and Madison raced after her. When Madison got to the side of the building, Ann was gone. All of the side doors were closed. Racing to the corner, she saw Ann's heels just before they disappeared again.

The gym was in the direction Ann was headed, and Madison bet that was where she'd find her. There were tons of places to hide in a gym. Madison took a gamble and streaked toward the scene of the scrimmage. She saw a door closing and grabbed the door handle at the last moment.

"Ann, stop!" she yelled as her friend skidded around the corner, using the polished linoleum floor like a skating rink. Madison followed Ann's lead and glided around the corner just as the door to the girls' locker room snapped shut. Madison pulled it open and dashed inside seconds before she heard a crash and her friend's scream. When Madison ran around the end of a row of lockers, she found Ann sprawled on the floor. Next to her was an overturned metal bucket the janitor had left in an aisle.

"Wow, girl, you're still faster than me," Madison said, gulping air as she walked toward her friend.

Ann looked miserable. She rolled over, sat up, and put her back against the nearest locker. Madison walked over to her.

"Why did you run? I've been frantic looking for you."

"I'm so sorry," Ann said. Her head was in her hands and she was near tears.

"Seriously. You've been here at Prescott-Mather? Why wouldn't you just call me?"

Ann looked up. "I was too embarrassed."

"Embarrassed? To go here?" Madison was confused and angry. "It's a really good school. I would have cared because we wouldn't be playing on the same soccer team, but we're best friends and I'd want what's best for you.

And knowing you're at a prep school is better than thinking that you've been kidnapped or are dead!"

"I didn't pick this school, okay? It's not my fault."

"What do you mean?"

"I just . . . " Ann's hands were clenched at her side in frustration. "I'm not just a student here. I'm in boarding school."

"Huh?"

"My parents are getting a divorce, okay?"

"What?" asked Madison, her anger melting away. "When? And what does that have to do with your being a student here? And in *boarding* school?" It was a lot for Madison to take in.

Ann sighed. "My parents had been having problems, and you know I went to Europe with my dad this summer." Madison nodded. "So he ended up getting a job there and just stayed."

"And your mom?"

"She didn't want to move to Europe or be with my dad. So they decided to divorce and she had a bit of a midlife crisis. She's 'working things out for herself' or something and living in a meditation/yoga retreat center. She put me here while she sorts things out."

"I saw your mom in Nordstrom the other day and she ran away from me."

"Yeah. She comes home some weekends. I needed

new clothes, so she ran to the mall before she came to see me."

"And she looked, well, different," said Madison thoughtfully.

"She's 'finding herself,' and her new self wears gypsy dresses and doesn't brush her hair." Madison giggled and Ann joined in. It felt good to have her friend back. "She ran away from you because I made her swear she wouldn't tell my friends about Prescott-Mather. She didn't know what to do when she saw you and she didn't want to lie, so she took off."

"Gosh, I'm sorry I upset her."

"It wasn't your fault, it was mine," Ann said.

"I stopped by your house and it looked like no one had been home in a while."

"Yeah, well, my mom needs to decide whether to stay in the house or move when she gets done with her meditative journey or whatever. I guess she's too busy with yoga and the retreat center to mow."

"I thought I saw a light in a second-floor room."

Ann blushed. "That was me. My mom dropped me off to get some stuff from my room while she went shopping for groceries. I saw you come up the walk and I hid so I wouldn't have to tell you what I was doing."

"Why didn't you tell me all this? I could have helped."

"I don't know. At first I felt bad complaining about

my family problems when you don't even have a mom. And then things just got worse and worse and it was too much to tell. I wanted to tell you. I can't have a cell phone here, dorm rules, and I was going to call during one of my mom's weekend visits, but after all this time I didn't know where to start."

"I wish you had told me. I'm your best friend," Madison said.

"I know, I was just really embarrassed to tell anyone about my problems, and especially that I'm going to Prescott-Mather after we'd spent so much time making fun of the kids who go here."

Madison gave Ann a big hug.

"There's nothing to be embarrassed about. A lot of our friends' parents are divorced. I would have helped you through it even if you have to go to a snobby school."

Ann laughed, but it was a nervous laugh, and Madison could see that her friend was still embarrassed and uncomfortable. Then Ann sobered.

"It sucks that we aren't playing soccer together," she said. "I feel like I deserted you. We had all those plans to win a championship. Now I'll probably be watching you win championships without me."

"We still can win championships. Just not this year. I'm only an alternate anyway. If your mom moves home, you can go to The Grove. Next year I should be starting, and we can wow everyone together. And there's always high school."

"I don't know if I'll be any good by then. I'm not playing this year because I was in Europe when they had tryouts."

"You're really good, Ann. A year off won't kill you. You'll take up where you left off when you decide to play again. And we'll still be on the club team together this summer."

Madison wrapped Ann up in another big hug.

"I am so glad I found you!"

"Me too," Ann said, hugging her back. Madison found herself grinning from ear to ear. One mystery was solved, just one more to go.

A BREAK IN THE SHELBY CASE

On Saturday afternoon, Ann took the bus from Prescott-Mather and met Madison on Northwest 23rd Avenue. Madison walked into Amore Pizza a few steps ahead of Ann. Jessi, Lacey, and Becca were in a booth eating.

Becca stared, her pizza slice suspended in front of her lips. Then she screamed, "OMG!"

Jessi rushed over and hugged Ann, exclaiming, "You're not dead!"

"Dead?" Ann answered, her confusion obvious.

"Madison thought you were dead or kidnapped," Lacey chimed in.

"Where were you?" they all asked at once.

Madison smiled and put an arm around Ann's shoulder. "Ann goes to school at Prescott-Mather," she said as they all found seats in the booth.

"Prescott-Mather?" Jessi asked.

"For boarding school. Ann's parents are sending her there because her dad moved to Europe and they're getting a divorce."

"Gee, I'm sorry," Lacey said.

"I'm just glad you weren't kidnapped," Becca said.

"Madison was driving us crazy with her nutty theories," Jessi said. "She had you tied up in a basement in Lithuania or some place like that."

Ann laughed. "That sounds like Maddy."

"She could have been kidnapped!" Madison said, offended to be the butt of a joke when she thought her theory was perfectly logical.

"I would rather be tied up in a basement in Lithuania than go to Prescott-Mather." Lacey laughed.

"Hey! It really isn't that bad. Some of the millionaires talk to me and the billionaires have stopped asking me to carry their books," Ann said. "All joking aside, though, the kids at Prescott aren't that different from the kids at The Grove. There are some mean kids and some extranice kids and the rest are okay."

Madison picked a slice of pizza from the metal tray and

ate it while the girls asked Ann about boarding school.

"Is it fun living in the dorms? No parents sounds like fun to me!" said Becca.

"It's a toss-up. There are even more rules than I had at home! Lights out, and curfews. And one TV for twenty girls!"

"Aargh!" Becca growled. "I'd never make it if I couldn't watch my shows."

"How did you find Ann?" Lacey asked Madison.

The girls ate pizza and drank Cokes while Madison told them why she'd tripped over the soccer ball during the scrimmage and about her trip to Prescott-Mather.

"Now that you've solved 'The Case of the Missing Best Friend,' how are you going to spend your free time?" Becca joked.

"I'm still working on the Shelby case," Madison said, suddenly serious.

"What's that?" Ann asked.

"My dad is defending Mark Shelby. He's accused of murdering Mrs. Shelby—our second grade teacher."

"Oh, my God, she's dead?"

"We don't know that. There's no body," Madison said.

Madison was about to continue when she thought of something so obvious that she felt like a dummy for not thinking of it before. When Ann went missing, Madison had jumped to the conclusion that she'd been kidnapped or murdered, but Ann had been *hiding*.

After they finished their pizza, the girls decided to go to the mall. It was great having the whole gang together, and it was especially great for Madison to see Ann be the same old Ann now that everyone knew her secret. Ann had told Madison she felt like someone had lifted a big weight from her shoulders as soon as she'd told Madison why she was at Prescott-Mather. The girls shopped a while before catching a chick flick at the cinema in the mall. Then Ann had to get back to Prescott-Mather. Only one thing spoiled the day for Madison. With the girls around, she didn't have a chance to tell Jake about her plan to solve the Shelby case.

Madison got home at ten and went straight to her room. As soon as she shut the door, she phoned Jake.

"I think I know what happened to Mrs. Shelby," she said excitedly.

"Spill," said Jake, who sounded instantly intrigued.

"What if Mrs. Shelby did the same thing Ann did?"

"You mean she's hiding?"

"Her car is missing, and so is her hairbrush and the other things I'd take with me if I was going on a trip. Miss Bauer was on the other side of her house making the call to see if Mrs. Shelby was okay. Then she called

911. Mrs. Shelby could have left without Miss Bauer seeing her!"

"What about the blood and the knife?" Jake asked.

"Remember the onion, the green pepper, the eggs, and the ham mentioned in the police report? I think Mrs. Shelby was making a Western omelet. Something Dad said at the bail hearing got me thinking. He made a joke about cutting his finger when he slices bagels. I bet Mrs. Shelby was so upset because she and Mr. Shelby argued that she gashed her finger while slicing the onion. That would explain the blood on the onion in the garbage and on the kitchen counter."

"And if they were arguing, Mrs. Shelby might have waved her hand around and sprayed blood on the refrigerator," Jake added excitedly. "And Mr. Shelby was too angry to notice."

"Then Mr. Shelby put his clubs in his car . . ."

"Which Miss Bauer thought was him moving the body to the car."

". . . and left on his golf trip."

"Which Miss Bauer interpreted as fleeing the scene of the crime."

"Exactly. When Mrs. Shelby ran upstairs to get a bandage and to pack, she was too busy to answer Miss Bauer's call. Then she drove off while Miss Bauer was on the other side of the house making the 911 call!"

Jake was quiet for a minute. "We still have a problem. If Mrs. Shelby ran away, why didn't she call the police after her husband was arrested? I can see someone getting mad after an argument and leaving the house, but why wouldn't Mrs. Shelby let the police know that she was alive when she learned that Mr. Shelby was facing life in prison for a murder charge?"

"That's something I can't answer, but Mrs. Shelby can tell us when we find her. That's the last piece of this puzzle. We have to figure out where she's hiding and convince her to come home and clear her husband. And I think I know how we can do that."

BACK FROM THE DEAD

During the ride to school on Monday, Hamilton mentioned that Judge Young had scheduled a hearing on his pretrial motions in the Shelby case for the next afternoon at three p.m. Madison was certain that she could solve the case if she was in the courtroom before the hearing ended. Soccer practice was over by four thirty. If she didn't shower and she sprinted to the courthouse, Madison thought she could make it.

Jake asked if he could go along after Madison told him her plan. The chance to solve a real murder case was too good to pass up.

☆ ☆ ☆

Jake and Madison were out of breath when they skid-ded to a stop in front of the courthouse on Tuesday after-noon.

"So, what's this hearing about?" Jake asked as they took the courthouse elevator to the fifth floor.

"You know that a person accused of committing a crime has a right to have a lawyer defend them."

"Sure."

"One way my dad makes certain that his client is get-ting a fair trial is by challenging evidence that the pros-ecutor wants to present to the jury if he thinks that the police got the evidence in a way that is forbidden by law or he believes that the rules of evidence forbid the DA from introducing the evidence. He can object to the evidence during the trial, but defense lawyers can also ask a judge to decide what evidence can be introduced before the trial starts. This saves time during the trial and avoids the risk that the jury will hear or see something they shouldn't. My dad filed a motion in Mark Shelby's case to keep out some of the evidence the DA wants to show the jury."

Madison was interested in the legal motion Hamilton had filed, but she had a more important reason for being in court. As soon as she and Jake walked into the court-room, Madison gave a silent fist pump. The woman she'd seen at the bail hearing and in the photo on the Shelbys' mantel was sitting in the last bench near the window.

Madison led Jake to seats on the other side of the courtroom from the mystery woman. Judge Young looked as mean as ever and appeared to be giving Hamilton a hard time. This was a good thing, because it meant her father would be concentrating on the judge and not looking around the courtroom.

Madison was certain that the mystery woman would lead her to Mrs. Shelby. When it looked like the hearing was winding down, Madison signaled to Jake and they slipped out of court.

The one part of her plan that Madison had not figured out was how she and Jake were going to follow the woman after she left the courthouse. If she walked it would be easy, but what if she had a car? Madison had money for a taxi, but taxis didn't cruise around the streets of Portland like they did in some big cities. Some parked at the big hotels near the courthouse, but Madison knew she would lose sight of her quarry in the time it would take to get to a taxi.

Fortunately, the mystery woman did not head for a parking garage. Instead she walked up Southwest Salmon Street. Portland has one of the best mass transit systems in the U.S., and Madison guessed that the mystery woman was headed for the trolley stop at Tenth Avenue. As she walked across town, the woman kept her eyes down and did not look around. She seemed preoccupied by deep thoughts, and Madison prayed that they would keep her from figuring out that she and Jake were tailing her.

Jake and Madison waited for the trolley on the end of the platform farthest from their quarry. When one of the blue cars stopped in front of them, they got on at the other end from where the woman entered.

The trolley rode into the Pearl District, a collection of highrise condos, upscale restaurants, and fancy boutiques. Madison spotted the mystery woman getting out, and she poked Jake. The two sleuths followed at a safe distance. Madison was prepared to duck into a doorway or pretend to look in a shop window the way she'd seen spies and private eyes do on TV, but it was never necessary.

The woman suddenly turned into the courtyard of a brand-new high rise and punched in an entry code. Madison raced forward just as the door opened. She hoped that the woman would not recognize her and Jake from court, and she got lucky.

"Thanks," Madison said as she and Jake walked in behind the woman, who just nodded. Madison peeked at her face. She looked worried. Madison decided that they were as good as invisible because the woman was completely focused on whatever was bothering her.

When the elevator stopped, Madison and Jake followed the woman down the hall and stopped at a door as soon as she stopped at another. The woman took a key out of her pocket, but the door opened before she could use it.

"What happened?" Madison heard a familiar voice ask. Madison felt a surge of adrenaline and relief rush through her body. "That's Mrs. Shelby," she whispered to Jake. She was alive!

They ran down the hall while the apartment door was still open. Madison skidded to a stop just as the mystery woman was about to go inside.

"Mrs. Shelby, remember me? Madison Kincaid, from your second-grade class at Lewis and Clark?"

Mrs. Shelby was dressed in sweat pants and a Portland Trailblazers T-shirt. Her hair was tied back in a ponytail. She looked thinner than Madison remembered, and she seemed confused.

"You followed me up here," the mystery woman accused the two sleuths.

"Actually, we followed you from the courthouse. It was the only way I could think of to find Mrs. Shelby."

"Why did you want to find me, Madison?" Mrs. Shelby asked.

"My dad is Hamilton Kincaid, Mr. Shelby's lawyer."

Mrs. Shelby looked frightened, and the two women

glanced at each other.

"You're not going to tell Mark where I am, are you?" Mrs. Shelby asked. Madison could hear the fear in her voice.

"I have to tell my dad," Madison said honestly. "Mr. Shelby is accused of killing you, but you're not dead. Once the DA finds out you're alive, he'll dismiss the murder charge against your husband."

"She's right," the other woman said. "This has gone on long enough, Ruth. Now that these two know you're alive, it doesn't make any sense to go on punishing Mark."

Mrs. Shelby folded her arms across her chest. Anger had replaced fear.

"We still don't know who you are," Jake told the mystery woman.

"I'm Sarah Tucker, Ruth's sister, and this is my condo."

"How did you know I was here?" Ruth Shelby asked Madison. She sounded suspicious and was glaring at her sister.

"Oh, Mrs. Tucker didn't tell anyone your secret. I deduced that you weren't dead from the evidence."

The two women listened carefully while Madison explained how she had solved the mystery of Mrs. Shelby's disappearance. When Madison finished, Ruth Shelby shook her head.

"You've grown up to become quite the detective,

young lady," she said. "I remember you being rather inquisitive when you were in my class."

"There's one mystery I still haven't solved," Madison said. "Will you tell me why you haven't cleared your husband's name?"

20

THE TRUTH COMES OUT

Judge Young had scheduled the hearing to start up again at nine o'clock the next morning. Madison, Jake, Mrs. Shelby, and her sister walked into Judge Young's courtroom shortly after court started. The district attorney was examining a policeman. Hamilton was taking careful notes, but the sound of the door opening made him and his client glance over their shoulders. Mark Shelby looked at his wife, returned his attention to the front of the room for a nanosecond, then leaped to his feet.

"It's her!" he yelled. "It's Ruth."

Judge Young pounded her gavel. "What's going on?" she asked. "Mr. Kincaid, get your client under control."

Mr. Shelby turned toward the judge. "That's my wife, Your Honor. She's not dead."

Judge Young, the DA, and everyone else in the courtroom stared at Ruth Shelby. The judge recovered immediately.

"Are you this man's wife?" she demanded.

"Yes, Your Honor," Ruth Shelby answered, clearly embarrassed by the attention she was receiving.

Judge Young smashed her gavel angrily. "This hearing is in recess. Bailiff, get the parties and that woman into my chambers immediately."

When Madison and Jake slipped into the judge's chambers behind Mrs. Shelby and Sarah Tucker, they found Madison's father and his client, the DA, the judge, a court reporter, and two deputies from the jail. Hamilton, who was sitting beside Mark Shelby, looked very upset.

Shelby jumped to his feet. "Where have you been?" he shouted. His face was scarlet, his fists were clenched, and every muscle in his body was knotted.

"Control your client, Mr. Kincaid. One more outburst and I'll have him cooling his heels in a jail cell."

Hamilton stood up and put a restraining hand on his client's forearm.

Sarah stepped between the Shelbys and stared angrily at her brother-in-law.

"Ruth has been hiding from you, Mark, because of the way you treat her."

"I spent time in jail. I was arrested."

"And you deserved everything you got," Sarah said. Then she turned to Judge Young.

"My sister ran away because Mark hit her. And it's not the first time. I told her she should tell the police she was alive after Mark was arrested, but she wanted him to suffer awhile so he would know how scared she is every time he loses his temper."

Hamilton looked at his client. "Is this true? Did you hit your wife the morning she disappeared?"

Mr. Shelby broke eye contact and looked at the floor.

"Sometimes I lose my temper," he mumbled. Madison could tell he was embarrassed to admit what he'd done.

"Not only is that no excuse," Judge Young said, "but hitting your wife is a crime—it's assault. You're angry that you had to sit in jail, but you could have gotten a much longer jail sentence if Mrs. Shelby had complained to the police. Consider yourself lucky that she hasn't had you arrested."

"Where did all the blood in the kitchen come from?" the DA asked.

"I was cutting an onion for a Western omelet when we started arguing. When Mark hit me, I cut my finger. I was waving my hand around when he stormed out and the blood went onto the refrigerator, the floor, and the counter. I threw out the bloody onion and ran upstairs to put on a bandage. While I was upstairs, I decided I'd had it with Mark's abuse and I packed and left."

Mark raised his head, but he couldn't look his wife in the eye. "I'm sorry, Ruth."

"You've said you were sorry before," Mrs. Shelby burst out, fighting back furious tears. "Then the next time you lost your temper you forgot you were sorry. If you don't want me to press charges, you have to take anger management classes."

"You're right," Mr. Shelby said. "I should have to prove I'll really change. I'll sign up tomorrow, first thing. I swear. I never meant to hurt you. Believe me." For the first time, Madison thought he seemed genuinely contrite. "I don't know what gets into me sometimes. And you got your point across. I was scared out of my mind when I was in jail, and I feel bad that I made you feel that way in your own home. I just want you to come back."

"Well, I won't. I don't believe you'll change. This last time was the final straw. I'm staying with Sarah and I'm not coming back."

Mr. Shelby hung his head. "Why did you even come in and clear me now?" he asked his wife.

Mrs. Shelby turned toward Madison. "This young lady convinced me that it was the right thing to do."

"How did you find Mrs. Shelby?" Judge Young asked.

Madison looked at Jake. He nodded at her, seeming to say, "Take it away," so Madison told everyone about her investigation. When she came to the part where she'd tricked Mr. Shelby into letting her into his house so she could see the photograph of Ruth and her sister more clearly, Mr. Shelby said, "I thought I'd seen you before."

Then Madison explained how she'd gotten the idea that Mrs. Shelby might be hiding after going to Prescott-Mather and learning that Ann hadn't been murdered but was only hiding from her friends because she was embarrassed about her parents' divorce.

A big grin appeared on Madison's face when she finished her explanation by telling the judge how she and Jake had followed Mrs. Shelby's sister. She was a hero, Madison told herself, and the reason she was a hero was because of her sleuthing abilities. Her father had to be so proud of her. Maybe she would be the greatest lawyer detective ever. She was certainly off to a good start.

Hamilton cleared his throat. "Did you pretend to have a cold so you could cut school and go to Prescott-Mather to look for Ann?" he asked.

Madison's grin disappeared. "I *had* to, Dad."

"And did you cut school today?"

"I had to," Madison said again, hearing her voice sound a bit desperate.

"Did you ever think of telling me your idea about following Mrs. Shelby's sister so I could put my professional investigator on Mrs. Tucker's tail?"

"Well . . . no, but—"

"Or telling me last night about finding Mrs. Shelby?"

"You never take me seriously, Dad, when I try to help you solve a case. So I decided to prove to you I *can* help by showing everyone just what happened in court, like Max Stone does in his books."

"I appreciate what you did for Mr. Shelby, but I'm grounding you for one week for cutting school and interfering in one of my cases after I specifically told you not to."

"If I hadn't snooped around, Mr. Shelby might have gone to prison for life."

"That's why I'm only punishing you for a week. But you have to learn that there are consequences for your actions."

"I had to find Mrs. Shelby on my own because you wouldn't have listened to me if I tried to talk about the case. You still think I'm a baby who doesn't understand a thing you do, but I'm in middle school and I'm *smart*, Dad. I want to help you, and I think I've just proved that I can."

Hamilton's brow furrowed, and he took a good look at his daughter.

"I guess you did."

"I can help you with other cases, too, if you'd just trust me."

"I do trust you, Madison. And you're right. I don't give you enough credit. I promise to take your ideas more seriously from now on."

"Are you still going to ground me?" Madison asked hopefully.

"Did you play hooky from school to go to Prescott-Mather and to come to court today?"

Madison colored and nodded.

"Then I have to ground you."

"Can I go to soccer practice?" She knew everyone was standing around listening, but she had to find out.

Hamilton thought for a moment. Then he nodded.

"The first game is this weekend. Can I play in it?"

"Yes, but don't expect to celebrate if you win. It's home for you as soon as the whistle blows. And I'll be there watching to make sure you behave yourself."

Judge Young had been listening carefully to the exchange between Hamilton and his daughter. When she saw that the lawyer was done, she smiled at Madison.

"I agree with your father. Playing hooky is serious. And going into strangers' houses is not a safe thing to do. But I also admire your brainwork. You showed great initiative, Madison. Maybe we can get you in here interning

162

when you're in high school—but just please promise me that you won't put yourself in harm's way again."

The judge's remark erased some of the sting of being grounded.

"I promise, Your Honor. Thank you," Madison said, her brain whirling. An internship at the courthouse would be a fantastic step on her way to law school . . . or maybe her own detective agency? Jake punched her arm, as if to say "congrats."

Judge Young looked at the district attorney. "Under the circumstances, Mr. Payne, I think a motion to dismiss is in order."

The DA nodded his head. "I'll do it right away, judge."

163

21

NOT BAD FOR A SEVENTH GRADER

The Grove's first regular-season girls' soccer game was against Reston Middle School. Madison knew she wouldn't start because she was an alternate, and she had little hope of getting into the game at all because of the way she'd screwed up in the scrimmage against Prescott-Mather. The coach hadn't even glanced in her direction throughout the whole game. Madison was resigned to riding the bench.

Ann, Jake, Becca, Lacey, Jessi, Peggy, and her dad were in the stands. Every once in a while she would look over her shoulder and someone would catch her eye and wave or give a thumbs-up to encourage her, but all that did was depress her because she knew they were just trying to cheer her up.

There were only a few minutes left till the end and the score was tied at one to one. This wasn't the time for a coach to put an untested seventh grader into the game. Then Carrie Metzger collapsed. She was the girl who had injured her ankle during the scrimmage at Prescott-Mather, opening a chance for Madison to play. Carrie's ankle had still been bothering her and she'd missed most of the practices the week before the game. She'd been playing on guts, but now she was rolling on the ground in agony and clutching her ankle.

The game stopped while Carrie was helped to the sidelines. Coach Davis looked at her bench for a moment. Then she pointed at Madison.

"Get in there for Metzger," she ordered. It took a second for Madison to realize that the coach was pointing at her.

"Yeah, you, Kincaid. Hop to it."

Madison jumped up and ran onto the field. Marci was giving the team a pep talk.

"There're less than three minutes left in the game and this is probably our last drive. Reston is one of the worst teams in the league, but we're playing like crap. If we tie we can kiss our chances to repeat as champion good-bye. So suck it up and let's show Reston what The Grove is made of."

The referee blew the whistle and Marci dribbled the ball downfield toward the Reston goal. Reston's defenders started moving toward Marci. Marci looked to her left toward one of her best friends and saw that she was covered. Then Marci looked right and saw Madison. It was just like the scrimmage. Marci and her friend had no shot and Madison had only one defender between her and the goal. Madison could read Marci's mind. Marci didn't like Madison and she had to be remembering Madison's unplanned flight through space that cost The Grove the win over Prescott-Mather. But Marci had no choice. Madison was the only player with a chance to win the game, so Marci gritted her teeth and passed the ball.

This time Madison didn't take her eye off it. She took off running. In the stands, her friends were on their feet, chanting, "Go, Madison, go!" The defenders who had been closing in on Marci started running toward her. There was still only one girl between her and the goal, but that wouldn't last long. If she was going to take her shot, it would have to be now. Madison was getting ready to try for the score when she saw Marci out of the corner of her eye. The eighth grader was suddenly all alone. Madison didn't think. She swiveled toward Marci and made a perfect pass.

All the defenders were running at Madison so quickly

that they couldn't change direction in time. It was down to Marci and the goalie and Marci would not be denied. She faked as if she was going to shoot into the right side of the goal. The goalie bit. The second she shifted, Marci sent a screamer into the left corner! The Grove girls went wild. Madison raced to join her jubilant teammates, and Marci smiled at her.

"That was a great pass, Kincaid," Marci said. Then she gave Madison a high five.

Too astonished to speak, Madison just grinned.

Ann and the other girls knew that Madison was grounded, so they said good-bye after the game. Hamilton told her he'd meet her in the parking lot. Jake was waiting for Madison when she walked out of the locker room.

"What a great pass!" Jake said. "Marci scored the goal, but you saved the day."

"Thanks, but I only played for a few minutes. I think it's a little early for the MVP award."

Marci and her gang barged through the swinging doors. Marci saw Madison and clapped her on the shoulder.

"Good game, Kincaid. See you at practice."

The other girls smiled and waved.

"Wow," Madison said. "Maybe I'll make it through the season alive after all."

Jake laughed. They walked out of the school. When Jake saw they were alone, he got serious.

"You know, it was hard for me to leave Georgia and move here, and try to make new friends and . . . well . . . I guess what I'm trying to say is I'm really enjoying soccer, but helping you solve the Shelby murder case is the most fun I've ever had."

"It *was* fun," Madison agreed, remembering all the ways Jake had helped her. And, if she was honest with herself, the fun she'd had just being around him. "And it was much better having you snoop with me than snooping on my own. We make a great detective team and should solve more cases together."

Jake looked like he wanted to say something when a Volvo station wagon drove up. "That's my mom. I've got to go."

"See you," Madison said. She felt shy but couldn't have explained why.

Halfway to the car, Jake turned back as if he'd forgotten something. He ran back to Madison, leaned over, and gave her a quick kiss.

"See you Monday," he said before jogging off.

Madison was too stunned to answer. She had never kissed a boy before. She put her hand to her lips and decided it was pretty nice. Walking toward the parking lot, she thought about the past few weeks. She'd started junior high, qualified for the best middle school soccer team in the city, found Ann, and solved a murder case. Now she might have a boyfriend. Not bad for a seventh grader.